HIGH LONESOME

HIGH LONESOME

LOUIS L'AMOUR

BANTAM BOOKS

TORONTO · NEW YORK · LONDON · SYDNEY

HIGH LONESOME
Bantam rack size edition / September 1962
Louis L'Amour Hardcover Collection / June 1981

Designed by Renée Gelman.

If you would be interested in receiving bookends for
The Louis L'Amour Collection,
please write to this address for information:

The Louis L'Amour Collection
Bantam Books
P.O. Box 956
Hicksville, NY 11801

ISBN 0-553-06202-6

Published simultaneously in the United States and Canada

Bantam Books are published by Bantam Books, a division of Bantam
Doubleday Dell Publishing Group, Inc. Its trademark, consisting of
the words "Bantam Books" and the portrayal of a rooster, is Regis-
terd in U.S. Patent and Trademark Office and in other countries,
Marca Registrada, Bantam Books, 666 Fifth Avenue, New York,
New York 10103.

PRINTED IN THE UNITED STATES OF AMERICA

10 9 8 7 6 5 4

**To three who told me
of the west when it was wild**

Jeff Milton
George Coe
Tom Pickett

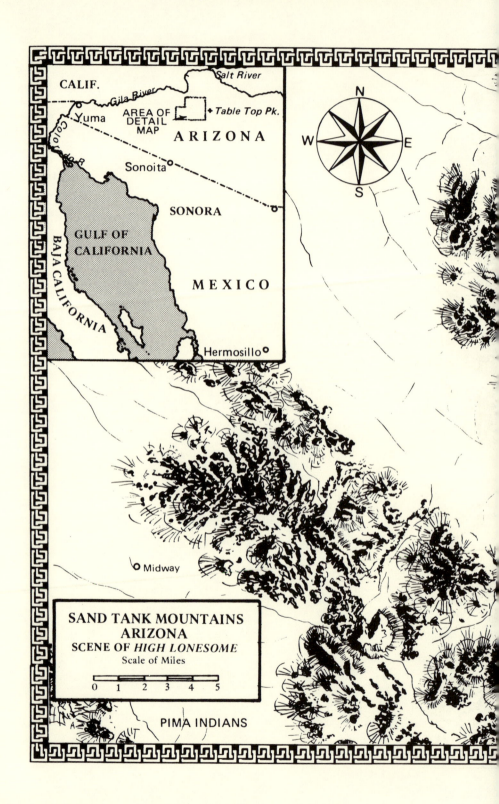

CALIF.

Salt River

Gila River

AREA OF
DETAIL
MAP

+ Table Top Pk.

Yuma

ARIZONA

Colorado R.

Sonoita

SONORA

GULF OF
CALIFORNIA

BAJA CALIFORNIA

MEXICO

Hermosillo

N

W E

S

Midway

**SAND TANK MOUNTAINS
ARIZONA
SCENE OF *HIGH LONESOME***
Scale of Miles

0 1 2 3 4 5

PIMA INDIANS

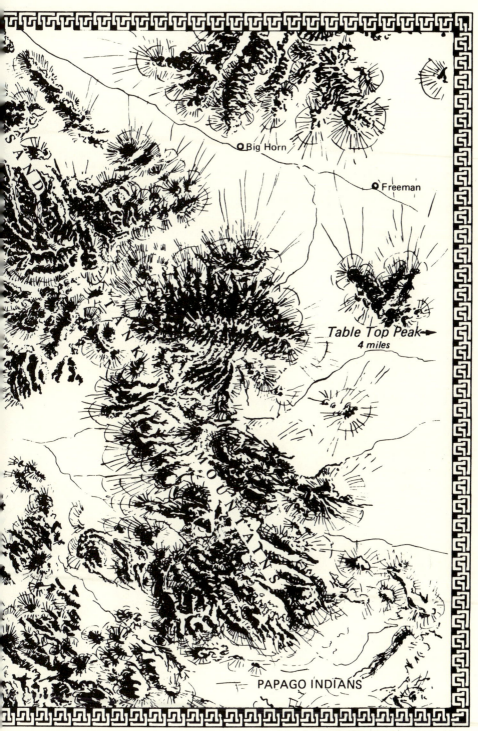

Big Horn

Freeman

Table Top Peak →
4 miles

PAPAGO INDIANS

Map by William and Alan McKnight

HIGH LONESOME

ONE

After the moon lowered itself behind the serrated ridge of the Gunsight Hills, two riders walked their horses from the breaks along the river.

The night was still. Only the crickets made their small music, and down by the livery stable a bay horse stamped restlessly, lifting his head, ears pricked.

Another rider, a big man who sat easy in the saddle, rode up out of a draw and walked his horse along the alleyway leading to the town's main street. Only the blacksmith heard the walking horse.

His eyes opened, for he was a man who had known much of Indian fighting, and they remained open and aware during the slow seconds while the horse walked by. Casually, he wondered what rider would be on the street at that hour of the night, but sleep claimed him and the rider was forgotten.

1

This rider did not emerge upon the street, but drew rein in the deepest shadows beside the general store, hearing the approach of the two riders coming along the street.

There was no sign of Considine, but he expected none. Considine had a way of getting to where he wanted to be without being seen.

The two riders went by, turning at the last minute in a perfect column right to stop before the bank. Each dismounted at once, and each held a rifle. Only when they were in position did Dutch walk his mount across the street and swing down in the comparative shelter of the bank building.

As he dismounted he held one hand carefully about a fruit jar. It was a very small jar, but Dutch treated it with respect.

Considine opened the bank door from within as Dutch brought his jar around the corner.

"It's an old box...nothing to worry about."

Dutch moved past him in the darkness, walking with the cat-footedness given to some very heavy men, and squatted before the big iron safe.

Considine walked back to the door for one last look down the empty street. Behind him the pete man had gone to work.

Hardy lit a cigarette and glanced over his shoulder. He was younger than Considine, and just as tall, but thinner—a knife-edged young man with a face that showed reckless and tough in the faint glow of the cigarette.

The Kiowa neither moved nor spoke. A blocky, square-built young man, he was a half-breed known from Colorado to Sonora, wanted everywhere and nowhere.

Considine walked back to where Dutch was working on the safe. Sweat beaded the big man's face as the steel drill bit into the softer iron of the safe. The first hole, at the top corner of the safe door, was well started.

"Spell you?"

2

"No."

Dutch was a craftsman and proud of his work. He had done time in the Texas pen for being caught with the wrong cattle, and while in prison he had learned from an old peterman how to crack a safe. Now there was no better man west of the Mississippi, but there was no hurry in him, not even under fire.

Minutes passed...up the street somewhere a door slammed, a moment of quiet followed, and then a pump complained wearily, and after an interval they could hear the water gushing into an empty tin bucket.

They waited, each man poised in position, Dutch resting the heavy drill on the floor. After a few minutes they heard a door close up the street, and then silence. Dutch replaced the drill in the hole and leaned into his job. Sweat trickled down his face, but he worked steadily, unhurried and confident.

Considine felt the pressure begin to mount. Every second they were here increased their danger. He knew these western towns only too well, and nobody got away with anything in any of them. He had heard gangs talk of taking towns, but it never happened. If a gunman or a pack of outlaws tried to tree a western town the population would vie to see who got the first shot.

Take the banker of this town, for example. He had been a colonel in the Union Army during the Civil War, and had been a lieutenant in the War with Mexico, and he had fought Indians and hunted buffalo....The saloonkeeper across the street was a noted buffalo hunter....The man who owned the general store had been the crack shot of his regiment during the Civil War, and had fought Indians in Wyoming and Nebraska.

The whole town was like that. Probably there weren't three men in town who had not used guns, and used them a lot. It was a time when every western town's population was made up of the daring, the adventurous, and the skilled. No tinhorn would ever tree a town like this, or any part of it. Gunmen and outlaws were left alone as long as they stayed with their kind, with the cheaper saloons and the girls of the bawdy houses.

An insect droned by in the darkness, and somewhere a quail called. Considine leaned against the door jamb and waited, listening to the sound of the drill.

He was a damned fool, he thought. Any man who tried to do anything like this was. How had he become a thief, anyway? He shied at the word thief. At first it had seemed a big lark. They had been out of money and wanted enough for a few days in town, so they bunched some cattle, drove them to a man they knew of, and sold them.

After that it happened again. On the fourth time they had been seen and there was a running gun battle and the only answer to that was to leave town.

He left ahead of a posse, and drifted to Kansas, and since then it had been just one thing after another until here he was, cracking the safe in a bank.

Four years of crime behind him, and he had made only a little more than he would have made working for wages on a cow outfit. With the difference that had he worked for wages, men would not be hunting him all over the country.

Dutch rested, mopping sweat from his forehead. The first hole was finished. Considine picked up a bar of home-made soap and began stopping up the crack around the safe door. Out in the street, one of the horses stamped and Dutch placed his drill in the new position and went to work. The iron showed white under the bite of the steel bit.

The quail called again, a lonely call, inquiring and plaintive. Considine slapped a mosquito on his neck and swore under his breath.

The pressure continued to mount. Hardy no longer leaned against the building. His nonchalance was gone.

4

He was sweating, too. Only the Kiowa seemed unperturbed.

Hardy hissed suddenly and Considine touched Dutch on the shoulder. The drill ceased to move and there was silence, and in the stillness Considine could hear the slow ticking of the bank clock.

On the cross street a few doors away they could hear two horses walking, two sleepy riders on sleepy horses. They crossed Main Street and vanished in the darkness, with the muzzles of two rifles on them all the way. When they had been gone a full minute, Considine spoke to Dutch and the big man returned to work. He had not so much as turned his head to look.

Time dragged. Considine grew impatient. His mouth was dry and he was getting jittery. The trouble was, that when a man took the wrong side of the law, every man was his enemy. You became fair game for any chance passerby who felt like taking a shot at you. You became an enemy of the public; but what was worse, the public became your enemy.

In the street a horse stamped again impatiently, and Hardy lit another cigarette. Dutch was through with his drill job, and he finished soaping the crack around the door. Then he made a cup of soap around the lock. To this he attached a short fuse.

Considine picked up an old mattress he had brought through the back door, and placed it against the safe. He wrapped the safe carefully in ragged blankets taken from the stable out back, and then he and Dutch opened all the bank windows so the concussion would not break the glass. The fall of broken glass had been known to awaken people when the concussion itself had not.

Considine went to the door. He glanced from the Kiowa to Hardy. "Ready?"

Each lifted a hand in assent. The Kiowa stepped out to stand with the horses, holding the reins of them all.

Considine glanced over his shoulder. "All right, Dutchman."

Outside, the watching men lifted their rifles, and the Kiowa murmured something to the horses. Dutch had lighted a cigarette, and now he touched it to the fuse. It hissed sharply and both men inside ducked out of the door and crouched close against the wall, waiting.

The quail called, its cry lost in the muffled boom from within the bank.

Dutch and Considine rushed the safe. The acrid smell bit at their nostrils. The door, blasted open, was hanging by one hinge.

Considine raked the contents of the safe to the floor, then swore bitterly. The heavy sacks of gold were gone!

There was only a tray full of coins. He dumped them into the sack Dutch held, ransacked a drawer and found a small package of bills—only a few dollars.

Somewhere down the street a door slammed, and instantly Hardy fired. The report racketed against the false-fronted stores, slapping back and forth across the narrow street.

There was a shout, then the heavy bellow of a buffalo gun. The Kiowa replied with a shot from his Winchester.

Considine straightened to his feet. "Nothing! Let's get out of here!"

Dutch crossed the floor in three great strides and ducked swiftly around the corner to his horse. Considine went out the back door, almost tripping over the crowbar with which he had sprung the door lock to gain entrance. From the street there was now a steady sound of firing.

Hardy was already in the saddle when Considine rounded the building, and the Kiowa had his bridle looped over his arm and was firing methodically up the street.

"All right!" said Considine.

The Indian stepped into the leather and the four riders wheeled into the deeper shadows of an alley. A window went up and a rifle barrel was thrust through at them, but Dutch put a .44 through the window glass and there came a startled yelp and the rifle fell to the ground outside.

The four riders scattered through the willows, splashed across the stream, then turned south and away. They did not ride fast, holding their horses for the necessary drive of speed should pursuit be organized in time to worry them.

Behind them in the town a few wild shots sounded, but by vanishing into the willows and crossing the stream they had taken themselves out of sight and out of range.

Considine held the steady pace for about two miles. Then he turned at right angles and rode into the stream, with the others following. They crossed it to a ledge of rock, then turned back into the stream and rode down-stream for a quarter of a mile, and came out on the far side and into the mouth of a sandy draw.

Tracks left in that deep sand were only dimples, shapeless and impossible to identify, or even to estimate as to the time they were made.

"How'd we do?"

Hardy was the youngest, and he was eager. He still believed that every score was going to be a big one. He had yet to learn that even the most carefully planned robberies might net exactly nothing...unless one counted the bullets fired.

"The gold was gone, all of it. There's maybe a couple of hundred in change and small bills."

"Hell!"

The opinion was scarcely open to debate, and nobody felt like talking. Even an empty bank does not like to have its safe blown up, and the citizenry would like the sport of the chase. In western towns—and Considine knew it all too well—there is often little excitement, so a bank robbery gives everybody a chance to have a fast ride and do a lot of shooting. A posse would be formed, and every man in it would be a tough, trail-seasoned veteran.

7

Considine led the way up the canyon as if it were broad daylight. When he felt the sudden added coolness in the air he knew they were at the seep, and turned sharply left. When he saw the notch in the skyline above them, he started his horse up the steep slide of talus.

It was a hard scramble for the horses, but it left no tracks, and at the top of the mesa they drew up to let the horses catch their wind. Pursuit would be relatively impossible until daylight, a good four hours off.

They rode until the sky was turning gray, and then Considine led them into a narrow draw, and up to a pole corral containing four horses. There was a shack with the roof and one wall caved in.

While Dutch made coffee and started breakfast, the Kiowa stripped the saddles from the horses they had ridden and turned the animals loose with a slap on the rump. They had been borrowed without permission and would return to their home range. He saddled the horses waiting in the corral.

Over the small fire they smoked and drank their coffee. Nobody felt like talking. The job had promised well and had failed, and now they were broke.

Nobody was hurt, nor had they hurt anybody. Had their escape been a few seconds slower or less carefully organized, one or more of them might now be dead. Of this they had no doubt.

"Well," Hardy said reluctantly, "even Jesse James pulled a couple of stick-ups that netted him nothing."

Nobody offered any reply, so he added, "But they say he buried a million dollars in a cave in Missouri. I'd sure like to find that."

"Don't you believe it," Dutch said. "Anybody who wants to can get the figures. In sixteen years of outlawry the James gang took in less than four hundred thousand, and that was split among six to twelve men. Hell, they were down and out most of the time."

"That safe was too easy," Dutch said. "I couldn't believe it."

They finished their coffee and got up. Dutch dumped out the coffee grounds and kicked dirt over the fire. They took a last careful look around to be sure nothing had been forgotten, and then mounted their own horses and rode out of the draw.

Considine was tired. His hard, spare body relaxed to the easy movements of his horse. His muscles ached with weariness and he desperately wanted to lie down somewhere under a tree and catch up on his sleep. That was always the trouble...everything a man wanted to do lay ahead of him.

Darkness retreated reluctantly into the hollows of the hills and hid under the spreading branches of the live oaks. The sun came up and grew hot. Considine paused when they topped out on a ridge and surveyed the country before them, shimmering with heat waves.

When a man took the outlaw trail he only thought of whooping it up and spending his time in the *cantinas*. He never thought of the long rides without sleep, of the scarce food, and the fact that he was a preferred target for any man's gun.

There had been a time...and it was then he thought of Obaro.

Considine never was far from thoughts of Obaro. The town was west and south, and was named for the ranch on whose range the town had begun—the O Bar O. It was a ranch that became a stage stop, then a supply point, and finally a town.

Considine had been a puncher on that ranch, and in the years there he had a friend, a girl, and a dream.

Pete Runyon had been his friend, a top hand on any man's outfit; and together, full of hell, they had ridden the range, working hard, playing hard, occasionally getting into brawls, sometimes with others, often with each other.

In those days there had been a lot of unbranded stock on the range, and occasionally when they wanted a night on the town they rounded up a few head of mavericks and drove them into town to sell. The trouble was that the big ranchers believed all stuff, unbranded or not, belonged to them.

Originally there had been a lot of cattle that were owned by nobody, and during the War between the States thousands of head had been left unbranded because the men were away at war. Afterward there was no way to trace title to any of that stock, and the big outfits claimed them.

Considine and Runyon were fired for selling stock, and warned off the range.

During the winter that followed the two lived on rustled stock. They rounded up unbranded stock, but now they were no longer too particular, and occasionally they caught up a few wearing brands.

Then Pete Runyon filed for the sheriff's office and was elected...and he married the girl.

Two nights later, Considine was waiting at a water tower for the Denver & Rio Grande train. He swung aboard, walked through the two passenger cars collecting from the passengers, and dropped off the train where a horse was waiting. A week later he got the same train on the way back.

South of the border he killed a man in a fight over a poker game and joined the Kiowa and Dutch. Four months later, Hardy joined them.

There was a bank in the town of Obaro that was usually well supplied with gold, and it was the boast of the townspeople that it had never been robbed. Robbery had been attempted on three different occasions, and they had created a special Boot Hill graveyard for the robbers. Seven men were buried there, and Considine knew all about that Boot Hill, for he had helped to bury the first man himself.

Every store and office in the town had its rifle or shotgun at hand, and any stranger was under suspicion if he approached the bank. It was the town's bank, and the people of the town intended to protect it. Anyone attempting to rob the Bank of Obaro must run a gauntlet of rifle fire...in a town notorious for its marksmanship.

The four rode steadily. Dutch was doing his own thinking. There was one thing in particular he liked about working with Considine. You always made a smooth getaway. No breakneck rides. Somehow he always managed to outguess the pursuit, and most of it was due to careful preparation beforehand.

Considine always made the beginning of the pursuit so tough that it broke the horses of the posses. Pursuit rarely lasted beyond the point where Considine would have the spare horses waiting.

The ride up that sandy draw, for example, and then up the rocky slide—that was enough to take the starch out of any horse. Nor could they ever be traced by their horses, for the horses used in the holdups were never their own mounts.

"Where to now?" Hardy asked.

"Honey's," Considine answered.

The Kiowa tilted his hat brim lower. Honey's place was not far from Obaro, and the Kiowa did not like Obaro. It was Pete Runyon's town, and Pete was a smart, tough sheriff. All the tougher because he had been an outlaw himself, and all the town knew it.

"Are you thinking of Obaro?" Hardy asked.

"Why not?"

Hardy grinned at the thought. "'Never was a horse that couldn't be rode, an' there never was a rider who couldn't be throwed.'"

Dutch squinted his eyes into the heat waves. The

11

horse that couldn't be ridden might throw a lot of riders before the last one rode it. The trick was to be the one who made the ride…only how did a man know?

And the town of Obaro, with Runyon for sheriff…it was a tough horse for any rider to top off.

TWO

In the Sand Tank Mountains there was a lonely corner unknown to the casual traveler. When Table Top Peak showed through a certain notch, the knowing rider would turn off the trail into the barren-looking hills.

Picking his way through the rocks and cacti, a rider could enter a box canyon and climb a trail that led out of it and up along the canyon's rim to a cirque, or hanging valley.

This was no more than a pocket, but here was usually good grass, and a dripping spring hidden behind a gnarled and ancient cedar. It was a place where several men might remain concealed, unseen even by a rider passing close by...although in the memory of those who knew of the place, no rider had ever come that close.

Three dim trails led from the pocket into the rough country of the Sand Tanks, trails by which a man on the dodge might swiftly lose himself.

"I reckon." He glanced at her. The wistful note in her voice worried him. "It's been lonely for you, ain't it, Lennie? You'd set store by neighbors now, wouldn't you?"

It wasn't right for a man to keep his daughter in a shack in a cow town. She needed to meet folks, to learn things from other women. She needed to meet some men, some decent men, and he was a mighty poor guide to such a trail.

Burt now, he had been a decent man. God knows he had been no angel, but decent around women, even if quick with a gun. Up to a point he'd been quick...trouble was, a man could never be sure when he wouldn't meet somebody who was quicker. Or when his gun wouldn't misfire.

A long time later, when she was huddled into her blankets, he bent over and pulled a couple of sticks back from the fire. It was dying down and he did not want it to burn any longer.

When he lay down he put his gun belt close at hand, with the butt where he could lay a hand on it. He stared up at the stars through the cedar branches, and then his eyes closed....

His eyes flared wide...only a few coals remained of the fire. Startled to awareness by an ancient sense of danger, he lay perfectly still, listening.

The moon was up, a half-moon partly hidden by foliage. At first he heard only water trickling, and then his ears identified the sound that had awakened him.

Riders....

He sat up and pulled on his boots. "Lennie?"

"I heard them, Pa."

By grabs, she was a girl! Never missed a trick. Well, he had never concealed the hard facts of life from her. She knew what danger was, and she had seen him kill one man...a man who had made an indecent remark to her. He was a brawny, hairy man, who made a brawny, hairy corpse because he had made such a remark, paying no attention to the grizzled wisp of a man at her side.

16

"Get dressed and stand to the horses."

Lennie drew her skirt to her and wriggled into it under the blankets. She was dressed as quickly as he was, and was standing by the horses to keep them quiet.

Dave Spanyer had a good view of the trail. For three hundred yards every inch of it could be covered from up here, but no posse had chased him in years, and he knew of no outlaws around who might know of this place.

Four riders....

They must have been traveling all night. There was something familiar about the way the second man sat his saddle, something about the bulk of his huge body.

Dutch...and riding second. Any outfit Dutch rode with had to be solid, and any man who led Dutch anywhere would be quite a man.

He watched them ride along the trail, and even in the moonlight he could see they rode better horses than any cowhand was likely to be riding. They were still some distance from the opening into the box canyon...were they coming here?

If that was Dutch, he knew of this place. Were they coming here, or riding on toward Obaro?

"We'll saddle up," he whispered to Lennie. He threw a saddle on the sorrel's back and reached under the belly for the girth. He felt the sorrel swell his belly and tried to stop him. The sorrel whinnied—caught some vague smell of horse, no doubt, a smell carried on the wind. And the harm was done.

He grabbed his rifle and crouched, waiting. It was quiet, too quiet. This was no job for one man, and Lennie, as if hearing his thought, slid her rifle from its scabbard and moved to the edge of the pocket.

Considine stood among the rocks on one of the back trails that led to the pocket and watched the girl take her position. With her first move he had recognized her as a woman. Now, with the sky lightening with the coming day, he could see her more clearly. He stepped out into the open and she turned sharply with the rifle on him.

"It's all right, I'm friendly," he said.

"Not if I can help it!" she said. Nevertheless, he could see her eyes were bright with interest or excitement.

Behind him he heard Dutch speak. " 'Lo, Dave. Figured you had cashed in a long time ago."

Dutch turned his head. "Come on in, boys. I know this old rawhider."

Considine looked at the girl. She was a beauty, really a beauty. "Did you hear that?" he said. "We're friends. Dutch knows your Pa."

"My Pa," she replied shortly, "knows a lot of folks I wouldn't mess with, so you walk in ahead of me and don't cut up any or your friend will have a friend to bury."

Considine was tall, lean, and raw-boned. His dark features were blunt but warm, and when he smiled his face lighted up. He smiled now.

"We'll walk in together. How'll that be?"

THREE

"He's all right," Dutch said, looking past the girl's head at Considine. "I rode with Spanyer."

Dutch gestured toward Considine. "Dave, meet Considine."

"Heard of him." The wary old eyes glanced at Considine and then away. Then Spanyer indicated his daughter. "This here's Lennie. She's my daughter. We're headin' for Californy."

Dave Spanyer was a slope-shouldered man who looked older than his years, but he was weather-beaten and trail-wise, and obviously not a man to take lightly. Considine knew the type. Most of them had come west early, as mountain men or prospectors, and they had lived hard, lonely lives, relying on their own abilities to survive.

"Going to marry her to some farmer?" Dutch asked.

"She ain't going to marry no outlaw, if that's what you

19

mean." Spanyer glanced at Considine, who was out of hearing. "If you're riding with him you'd better fight shy of Obaro."

"You don't know him."

"I know Pete Runyon." Spanyer looked toward his daughter, who had walked over to their horses. It was growing light now, and a good time to move on. "Don't say you weren't warned."

Dave Spanyer watched them ride on, walking to the edge of the trail to watch them go. Lennie came up beside him.

"Stay away from men like that, Lennie. They're no good. There's not many of these new outfits that are worth riding with, but these men...Well, I don't say they ain't good men in their way. That Dutch, I knew him a long time back, and Considine, everybody knows him."

Spanyer turned away. They could have it. They could have the long, cold rides, the lonely camps, the scarce rations. All he wanted was a place in California in the sunshine where he could raise horses and some of that fruit he had heard tell of.

"He's handsome, Pa. The tall one, I mean."

"None of that! Don't you be gettin' any ideas, now. He ain't your kind."

Considine was a fool to go back to Obaro, or any place close to it. Nobody had ever tapped that bank and nobody was likely to, not with Runyon the sheriff. And he had a town full of tough men.

Spanyer turned his mind to California. He knew where he was going out there, knew the place well because he had got off a stage there once. It was a little place called Agua Caliente, tucked in a corner of the San Jacintos, and he had laid up there several weeks when he wanted to stay out of sight.

Riding the outlaw trail was all right for the young sprouts, but a man was a fool to stay with it. He would buy

20

a little place from the Indians, irrigate a patch, and raise some fruit. It wasn't likely that anybody would show up around there who was likely to know him, and after a while he would move on out to the coast if things looked good. By that time they would have forgotten him.

"Those men were outlaws, weren't they?"

"It doesn't matter. Don't you pay them no mind."

They mounted up, and when he was in the saddle he said, "Never pays to know too much. You didn't see anybody, you don't know anything about anybody."

Dave Spanyer turned his thoughts from Considine and his men and thought of the trail ahead. It was Indian country, and he was foolish to try to get through alone. Still, no Indian knew more about the trails than he did, and if necessary he knew how to live off the country.

He was taking a chance, especially with Lennie along, but they had nothing back where they came from, and folks had found out about him. The daughter of an outlaw would have no chance to grow up and live a decent life; but out there in California...well, most of his kind stayed in Arizona. In fact, unless they were sent to Yuma pen they never went as far west as the Colorado.

He rode a few yards ahead of Lennie, his Winchester in his hand. He knew the desert too well to be fooled by its seeming innocence. If all went well they would noon at Pozo Redondo. There was a store there, and he could buy what supplies they needed before going on into the desert.

With Considine and his outfit in the vicinity, it would be a good idea to stay away from Obaro. Somebody might remember his connection with Dutch and he would be involved.

The sun came up over the ridge and it grew hot. Nothing moved out on the wide sagebrush flats. Suddenly he saw the tracks...four unshod ponies had crossed the trail...hours before.

21

Dave Spanyer stared off in the direction they had gone, but there was nothing out there that he could see, nothing at all.

At the foot of Wildhorse Mesa is a spring, and around it some ancient cottonwoods offer their shade. Once deer had come here to drink, but they came no longer, for in the shade of the trees there was now a combination store, stage stop, and saloon owned by "Honey" Chavez.

When he first came to the country Chavez had made a business of robbing the desert bees and selling their honey in the settlements, hence the nickname.

The store building was eighty feet long and twenty feet wide. It was built of adobe, and facing it across what was humorously called the "plaza" was another building almost identical in size which was a bunkhouse carrying a faded sign: BEDS—Two Bits.

Honey Chavez was fat, sloppy, and nondescript, but there was little going on which he did not know about, for he was a man who listened well and found means to profit by the information he gathered. Despite his appearance, he was a man who had many times proved his courage against the Apaches, although usually he was on friendly terms with them. Lacking most of the virtues, Honey Chavez had one very necessary one—he knew when not to talk.

From the porch in front of the store there was a good view both up and down the trail, while behind the place was a towering mountain that closed off all approach. In front of the place and across the trail the desert stretched away into almost endless distance before reaching some haunting blue hills, far, far away.

Considine led the small cavalcade into the plaza, where they dismounted and tied their horses. Chavez was standing in his doorway, scratching his fat stomach and watching them. "Getting close to Obaro, ain't you?"

Considine ignored him. Everybody knew about his relationship with Pete Runyon, and what could be expected if he returned to Obaro.

He glanced up the trail. There was no sign of Dave Spanyer and his daughter. He stared that way, almost hopefully. She had been quite a girl. And that old man of hers—he was a tough old man, a very tough old man, but they should not be riding through Apache country alone.

Dutch stopped beside him. "Don't worry about them, Considine. That old man is no fool."

"You saw those tracks."

"He'll see them, too."

The Kiowa led the horse to the trough for water, then to the corral. Considine watched him gloomily. The Kiowa was lucky, for he never seemed to think about things or to have any worries beyond the moment—but that might be an illusion.

"The trouble with me is," Considine said aloud, "I think too much."

Dutch nodded his big head. "You're the best in this business, Considine, but you ain't cut out for it. I never knew a man who was less cut out for it. To me this comes natural and easy, but not to you. The very thing that makes you good at this business shows you don't belong in it. You've got an instinct to watch out for the other fellow...you don't care how much grief you shoulder yourself as long as you can keep others out of trouble. That's why you plan so carefully. That's why you're worrying about Spanyer and his girl now."

"Maybe."

Perhaps it was true, yet if so, his presence here was a contradiction, for his only reason for being here would be that bank in Obaro. The only obvious reason...Part of it was that everything about Obaro rankled, and it was not only Pete Runyon and the girl he'd married—it was the town, all of them.

He glanced around at Chavez. "You been to town lately?"

"Two weeks ago...maybe three."

"You'd better go in and have a look around."

Chavez rubbed his fat hands on his pants and shifted his eyes uneasily. In a way, he was afraid of Considine, for the big, quiet man was very sure of himself, and was known to be a dangerous man with a gun. But Chavez was afraid of Runyon, too.

Chavez did business with the wild bunch. Any outlaw could stop off here, buy supplies, pick up information, and never worry about anything being said. It was a safe place—as safe as any man living beyond the law can find; but Honey Chavez was no fool, and he had been careful not to cross Sheriff Pete Runyon.

"It's your business...but have you thought about this?" His big round eyes searched Considine's face. "There will be much trouble."

Irritation showed in Considine's face. "Are you riding in? Or do I go myself?"

"It is time for me to go. They will expect me to come about now, for there are supplies I must get." He hitched up his sagging pants. "I will see what I can find out."

He walked to the flea-bitten roan at the hitch rail. Sure, he reflected, Considine can pull this holdup and ride on, but I have to stay here, and Runyon will come looking for me.

Runyon would close him up, drive him out. At the very least. Honey Chavez swung into the saddle and rode away...a very thoughtful man.

Considine went into the store and the others followed. Picking up a newspaper, he dropped into Honey's chair.

Where was it a man made the switch? Had it really been back there in Obaro when Mary chose Runyon instead of him? Or had he actually made the switch even before that?

Coming here was a fool thing, but they needed money and the money they needed was in Obaro. With a few sacks of gold they could run for the border; and with the Apaches out, there was small chance of pursuit. That was one of the things on which he was counting. Obaro was an exposed town, and the good family men who lived there would not want to run off into the desert and leave their wives, children, and property unprotected.

There must be no killing. He would like to rob the bank of Obaro to get the money and to taunt them, but he wanted no killing. Aside from the fact that he hated no one there, there was a practical side. Take their money and they might come after you; but kill a friend of theirs and they would follow you through hell.

It had come to his attention that men with money in the bank rarely rode in posses. Or maybe his viewpoint was sour.

Nobody knew better how tough Obaro could be. As such towns went, it was an old town...fourteen years old, to be exact. And it might even last another ten.

In the first year of the settlement's existence the Apaches had raided it nine times, and the second year fourteen times. They had driven off stock, burned out-lying buildings, and in the first few years of the town's existence had killed twenty-six men and a woman within three miles of the town.

Considine knew how eagerly the town awaited an attempt at bank robbery. Unless there was an Indian attack—which was considered a normal part of the day-to-day life—the only excitement they had was a robbery attempt, and Considine himself had helped to handle one such.

He grinned at the thought of outwitting Runyon and carrying off the robbery. Runyon was the only man who had ever whipped him in a stand-up and knock-down fight, and until the last minute it had been close. Both of them had been knocked down half a dozen times, both were

25

bloody, and then Runyon had caught him with that right-hand punch.

Pete Runyon was somewhat heavier, but a fast man for his weight, and he knew how to scrap. They had fought before that, with honors about even, but that last fight had not been for fun or over a minor grudge. They had, in effect, been fighting over Mary. And Runyon had whipped him.

Considine knew what he really wanted was to fight Runyon again, but there would be no time for that. They would have to plan this one with infinite care.

Once they had the money they could make a run for the border, but this time there would be no boozing in the *cantinas*. At least, not for him. He would buy a small ranch and hire some Basques to work for him, for they were good, steady men and hard workers, and they would make money for him.

The store smelled of drygoods, of calico and gingham, of new leather and gun oil, of tobacco and spices. There was a rack of new Winchesters, a couple of second-hand Spencers, a case containing some new six-shooters, and the usual odds and ends of gear and supplies to be found around any frontier trading post.

Dutch cut off a piece of cheese with his jackknife and walked over to where Considine was seated. He hitched himself up on a barrel. "It should be rich," Dutch said, "but this is a tough one."

Dutch had thought about this before. Months ago he had come into Obaro and stopped there briefly. No one knew him there, and he had loafed about town listening to the gossip. He had even gone into the bank to change some money, and had glanced at the safe. It was not too tough. It could be done.

There was still much talk in the town about the great fight between Runyon and Considine, and there were many who thought that if it happened again, Runyon would not be so lucky.

Of the four of them, only Considine would be known in town, so if necessary the others could ride in and be located about town before anything was suspected. That depended on whether they wanted to take the bank in broad daylight or in darkness.

Considine got up. "You boys talk it over, then I'll lay it out for you."

He went outside and stood at the end of the porch looking down the trail.

It was very hot. A dust devil danced in the distance, the sky was wide and empty, the bunch grass barrens stretched away to the mountains. Far down the trail among the dancing heat waves he saw two riders, unbelievably tall in the mirage made by the shimmering heat.

That would be Dave Spanyer and his girl. What had he called her? Lennie...

When she had looked at him there had been something very wise, very knowing in her glance, but it was that unconscious awareness such girls sometimes have, old as the world, old as time.

But this was no time to be thinking of a girl, especially when her father was a tough old coot like Dave Spanyer. They said he had been a gunman for the big cattle outfits, and had killed eleven men. That might be an exaggeration, for many such stories were exaggerated, but he was no man to fool around with.

Considine went to the pool and dipped up a bucket of water, and then went back among the trees and stripped off his clothes and bathed, dipping another bucket to complete the job. He discarded his old shirt, and went back to the store for another.

Dave Spanyer and Lennie were riding into the yard as he crossed to the store, and he saw the girl look at his broad, powerfully muscled shoulders, and then at his eyes.

He went into the store and selected a dark red shirt with pearl buttons from the stock, and slipped it on. When

27

he came out again, Spanyer was taking the horses to the corral.

Spanyer came up on the porch with Lennie, who carefully kept her eyes averted from Considine. She was, he admitted again, quite a girl. And the fact that her blouse was a bit too small for her did nothing to conceal the fact.

"Where's Honey?" Spanyer demanded.

"Gone to Obaro."

They went inside, and after a moment Considine followed. The Kiowa was balancing a knife in the palm of his hand, and as they entered he suddenly caught it by the tip and flipped it into the calendar across the room. It stuck there, and quivered.

It was June, 1881.

FOUR

It was still and hot. Outside a road runner appeared and darted along the road, slowed, flipping its tail up and down, then ran off a little farther. A mockingbird sang in a cottonwood tree back of the store.

A buckboard went by on the trail, flanked by two riders, but it did not stop, making fast time along the road to Obaro.

"Never figured you to have a family, Dave," Dutch said, glancing at Lennie; "and she's no youngster, either."

"She's been to school in Texas," Spanyer replied proudly. "More than you and me can say."

"You should find a place and roost, Dave. This is no time to be traveling—not with a girl along."

"We'll make it." Then irritably, he added, "I figured on going into Obaro, but now I dasn't...they might figure I was riding with you boys and I'd be on the run again."

"Sorry."

Considine went outside again, and Lennie watched him go, nettled that he had made no attempt to talk to her. She was very curious about him...he was so quiet, and sort of stern.

Spanyer looked after him. "Is he as good as they say?"

Dutch nodded. "Better...he's as good as any of them ever were, Dave, and you know I've seen them all—Courtright, Allison, Hardin, Hickok, Stoudenmire, Pink Higgins, all of them."

"Then why doesn't he ride into Obaro and shoot it out with Runyon?"

"He could beat Runyon with guns and they both know it, but he wants to whip him with his hands because that's the way they've always fought."

"He's crazy...plumb crazy."

"They used to ride together. They were saddle partners."

Spanyer shrugged. "Hell, man, that's different."

Considine stood alone near the corral. What was the matter with him? He could not recall feeling this way before, and it irritated him. There was a nameless restlessness on him, something for which he could not account.

Was it because he was so close to Obaro? Was it because Mary was not far away? Or was there something else in him which he did not know?

Recent rains promised water in the *tinajas*, the natural tanks in the rocks along the trail they would follow into Mexico. Honey Chavez would arrange for the horses to be waiting for them in the box canyon, and they could make the switch there and have a good running start. Long ago he had scouted that country in company with a Papago who knew the desert wells and the *tinajas*, and Considine had mapped those places in his mind.

Due south of the box canyon there were *tinajas* that should contain just enough water for their horses and them-

30

selves, and their visit would empty them; from there on a posse pursuing them would be waterless. But every mile would be alive with danger, for the Indians would be on the move.

However, leaving the chance of Indians out of it, the plan for the getaway was as close to fool-proof as any such plan could be.

He went over it again, considering every aspect. It was simple, and that was what he liked best of all. There was nothing that could go wrong. Chavez would have the horses there—he would personally see that he did—and if the escape from town was clean, the rest should work like a charm.

The problem of the town remained. Unless they could draw all the people away from the main street there would be small chance, for armed strangers riding into Obaro would arouse immediate suspicion. But he had an idea how he would manage that.

Honey Chavez should be back soon, and knowing Honey, Considine was sure he would have all the information they needed, for Chavez had long since proved himself an expert at this sort of thing.

Considine's thoughts reverted to Mary. She had chosen wisely, even though he had hated her at the time. Pete had settled down. He was sheriff, but he was running a few cattle, too, and was becoming a man of some importance in Obaro and the surrounding country.

Mary was a tall, pale girl. She was blonde, she was intelligent, and she was lovely, yet somehow he had difficulty in remembering just what she looked like. He told himself that was nonsense, but the fact remained that his recollection of her was no longer distinct. Had he really been in love with her? Or was it merely that his pride was hurt that she jilted him for his friend?

Folks said time was a healer, but time was also a thief. It robbed a man of years, and robbed him of memories.

This would be his last ride in the night, his last run for the border. He was going to have that Mexican ranch; the others could do as they wished.

The wind skittered dried leaves along the ground, and he looked up quickly. There was a faint coolness on the wind...back in the hills there was a rumble of thunder.

Honey Chavez rode in an hour later when the sun had dropped below the horizon. Considine walked out to meet him, and took the heavy sack from his hands. Honey swung down and turned his back to the horse.

"Apaches killed two men and burned a place over east." He glanced toward the store. "Who's that inside?"

"Dave Spanyer and his daughter."

"*Spanyer?*" Chavez looked at him quickly. "Is he with you?"

"He's quit. He's headed for California with his daughter."

"This here is no time to travel with a female."

"Well," Considine said sharply, "what about it?"

"The mine has a pay roll at the bank—thirty thousand. There will be twice that much, all told."

Thunder rolled, and a gust of wind whipped dust into a cloud. There was a brief spatter of rain, and both men started for the barn with the Chavez horse.

"To go into town we'll need four horses that nobody knows. We'll leave our own in the box canyon, and when we get to them we'll turn yours loose."

"Sounds all right." Chavez stripped the saddle from his horse and placed it astride a sawhorse in an empty stall. "I saw Runyon. He looks fit."

Leave it to Pete. He knew Considine would be coming back some day and knew they would settle it with their fists, so he was ready. Pete had always been ready, when it came to that. Considine remembered the time his own horse lost its footing on a narrow mountain trail and started over the edge. Pete Runyon's rope had come out of nowhere and dropped over his shoulders just as he was going past the edge. It had been a quick bit of business.

Runyon had saved his life on other occasions, too, and Considine had done as much for him. It was nothing they ever talked about, except in joking, for it was all in the day's work, and was accepted as such.

He could hear the soft laughter of Lennie Spanyer inside the store. She was talking to somebody—Hardy, probably. For a moment he felt a flash of jealousy, and it surprised him. He had not thought that seriously of any girl since Mary...not to say there had been no other girls. There had been a good many, most of them below the border, but he had been careful not to grow too concerned.

Rain came suddenly, and it came hard. The two men ran for the store and stopped on the porch, listening to the roar of the rain on the roof. It was a regular old-time gully-washer. This might complicate things a little if the rain lasted long enough to leave water along the trails.

From the dry earth there arose that strange odor he knew so well, that peculiar smell of long-parched earth when first touched by rain.

On the porch the two stood together, and after a minute Chavez said, "The stuff is there, all right, no question about it. When I went to the bank they were counting the gold into sacks."

"Hear anything else?"

"I was curious...so I started talk about the fight between you and Runyon. That started an argument... everybody takes sides on that fight."

"Did you mention my name?"

"No...I don't think so."

It might have been any cow-country general store at that hour, with rain on the roof and the Kiowa sitting at a table under a coal-oil lamp idly shuffling a pack of cards

33

in his big brown hands. Dutch and Spanyer sat at one side on the counter, swapping stories of the old days.

Hardy cornered Chavez as the two men entered and went off in a corner, arguing with him.

They might have been any group of cowhands waiting for the rain to pass, but tomorrow there would be quick, fateful movements, a thunder of hoofs, perhaps the thunder of guns. Tomorrow they would be riding into Obaro, the town that was the nemesis of outlaws.

Considine watched, fascinated at the flowing, smooth movements of the Kiowa's brown hands. The man was a marvel with cards.... The old scar on the half-breed's face stood sharply clear under the lamp.

Spanyer turned to Chavez. "Owe you for supper."

"That's all right. You're a friend of Dutch. You forget it."

He took a package from the counter and handed it to Lennie.

"What the devil is that?" Spanyer demanded.

Chavez shrugged his fat shoulders. "A present from Hardy here."

Spanyer's lips thinned down, and he ripped open the package, exposing several folds of cloth Lennie had admired earlier. Abruptly he thrust the package back at Chavez, then he turned on Hardy.

"When my girl needs clothes, I'll buy them. Your kind will throw a brand on anything you can. Stay away from her, you hear me?"

"Take it easy...old man." Hardy's tone was careless, and he underlined the "old man" with faint contempt.

Spanyer's face stiffened. "Why, you dirty pup!"

Hardy's hand dropped for his gun, but Dutch was too quick. He grabbed Hardy, then stepped between them, stopping the half-drawn gun.

Hardy wrenched at the hand, trying to tear free, but aware that Spanyer's gun had come smoothly into position.

"He's too fast for you, Hardy," Dutch said. "Lay off!"

Hardy was suddenly very still. Over Dutch's shoulder he looked into the slate-gray, icy eyes of the old man and saw no mercy there. Something within him seemed to shrink back. He was afraid of no man, but he knew death when he saw it. Only Dutch's intervention had saved him. He had never seen a gun drawn so fast before—except by Considine.

"He didn't mean any harm!" Lennie protested. "He was just trying to be nice."

"Get over there to your room!" Spanyer gestured toward the building across the plaza.

Lennie's face flushed, but she turned obediently. She walked out of the door, and Spanyer holstered his gun. His eyes went around their faces, coolly measuring them, and then he followed his daughter.

Hardy stood silent for several seconds, and his anger evaporated—his anger and his surprise.

"Thanks," he said suddenly. "Thanks, Dutch."

"Forget it," Dutch said, then he added in a mild tone, "That's a tough old man, so don't think you've lost your grip. I'd never try him with a gun, I know that."

The Kiowa shuffled the cards, the flutter of the deck the only sound in the stillness of the store. Dutch picked up his blankets and started across the plaza, and after a minute Hardy followed.

They were all tense, for the realization of tomorrow was upon them all.

Rolled in her blankets in the room with her father, Lennie stared wide-eyed and sleepless at the darkness above her. She was not thinking of the excitement of the near shooting, but of Considine.

She had never known a man like him—he was so quiet and self-contained, almost brooding. And, despite the fact that he was an outlaw, she knew her father respected him—and Dave Spanyer respected few men.

On the trail after their meeting at the spring in the old outlaw hide-out her father had warned her: "They ain't no good, Lennie, and it's a fool thing that Considine has in mind. They'll get themselves killed, and nothing more."

Restlessly, she turned over and tried to go to sleep. In spite of the rain it was still hot. Water dripped from the eaves outside, and the room smelled of soiled bedding and damp walls. She turned and twisted, and at last she sat up.

Her father was asleep, and she looked toward him in the darkness, feeling a vast pity for him. He tried so hard, but he knew so little of how to be tender or gentle with her. Yet it was in him to want to be gentle. Was Considine like that?

It was close in the tightly shut room, and she felt stifled. Rising with infinite care—even though her father slept more soundly in these days—she went to the door wearing only her flimsy shift. She glanced once more toward her father, and then eased open the door and stepped out on the long veranda.

After the hot, stuffy room the rain was cool and pleasant. She crossed the yard toward the stable, liking the feel of the mud between her toes, as she had when she was a little girl. Often when lonely she came to the horses, filled with the need to give affection and tenderness.

A flash of lightning revealed low, massive thunderheads above the mesa's black rim. Somewhere above the storm clouds the moon was out, and a diffused grayness lay over the rainscape.

She walked to the barn and entered. The horses rolled their eyes at her, snorting gently in mock terror. She could see the white of their eyeballs in the vague light within the barn. She whispered to them and rubbed the neck of her mare.

The mare's head bobbed suddenly, and Lennie turned swiftly to see Considine come through the curtain of rain and into the barn. She drew back against the stall's side, frightened.

"You shouldn't be out here at this hour, Lennie." He spoke quietly, and her fears left her. "This is Apache country."

"It was so hot and stuffy," she said.

"I know...but you can never tell about Apaches. They don't like to fight at night, but that doesn't keep them from prowling."

She had no words with which to respond, and she stood there, wanting to say something, to break down the wall between them, to let him see that she was a woman, to feel the tenderness she suspected lay within him. She had talked with few men, and those few were friends of her father's, and older than she.

"I shouldn't be talking to you," he said gloomily. "I'm no kind of a man to talk to a girl like you."

"I...I like you."

She said it hesitantly, feeling herself blush at saying such a thing to a man she scarcely knew. It was the first time she had said that to any man, and she was very still inside herself with the wonder of it.

"I'm an outlaw."

"I know."

They stood together, facing each other, only a few feet apart, and on the roof above them the rain fell with a pleasant, soothing sound. The thunder had retreated sullenly into the canyons where it muttered and grumbled.

She shivered.

"You're cold," he said. "You'd better go in."

But she did not move to go, and he took her in his arms and kissed her gently on the lips. She held very still, trembling and frightened, yet liking it, and wanting him to hold her closer.

Outside the rain whispered and something moved. He

37

reached behind him, feeling for the pitchfork. She had felt his hand leave her side, but had not divined its purpose.

"Afterwards...what will you do?"

"Go to Mexico."

She knew about Mexico. Her father had told her that long ago men in trouble always went to Texas, but now they went to Mexico. Her father and mother had lived there before she was born.

"Will you ever come back?"

"Maybe...I don't think so."

He was listening, but there had been no further sound. Had he really heard something? He considered it, and knew there had been a sound that was not of the rain and the night.

He turned around, lifting the pitchfork. He cursed himself for a fool, so preoccupied with the girl that he had come out without a gun.

Suddenly a man stepped into the barn and faced them. It was Dave Spanyer, and he had a gun in his hand.

He gestured at Lennie. "You! Get to the room!"

As she went by him he said from the corner of his mouth, "And get dressed. We're pullin' out."

Considine stood still, holding the pitchfork in his hand, but realizing he would not use it against this man, for he held nothing against him, and he could understand how it must seem to him.

"Next time I see you," Spanyer said, "you be wearin' a gun."

"You're jumping to conclusions," Considine said quietly. "There was nothing wrong. She came out to be with the horses, and I was afraid there might be Indians around."

"You heard me."

Dave Spanyer backed to the door and stepped out, and then there was only darkness and the falling rain.

FIVE

There are no dawns like the dawns that come to desert lands, nor are there colors anywhere like the pastels of the wastelands. There is no atmosphere anywhere with half the sharp clarity of the desert air following a rain—and no land holds death so close, so ready, so waiting.

Now the rain was over, the dry washes had carried away the weight of water, their swift torrents running away to leave their sands once more exposed to the relentless heat of the sun. Only the desert plants were greener, and the countless tiny roots that lay just beneath the surface had drunk greedily of the sudden rush of desert water.

Nowhere is survival so sharply geared to the changes of weather. Seeds lie dormant, mixed with the sand; a little rain falls, and nothing happens, for the water that has fallen is not enough for the seed to sprout. Within the seed some delicate mechanism awaits sufficient water; then suddenly, when it comes, the seed sprouts and grows, other plants

39

put out their quick leaves, and for the moment the desert is alive, glowing, beautiful.

This morning the tracks of animals and birds were sharp on the unblemished sand, but there were no tracks of horses nor of men. Dave Spanyer's cold eyes swung to the hills, searching for smokes, the talking smokes of the Indian that might carry word of his passing.

He was a worried man. He had been brusque with Lennie, and he was sorry for it now; but he had a way of forgetting that she was no longer a child, that she was a young lady, and of an age when she would be thinking of a man. Yet "lady" was the key word in his thinking. Her mother had been a lady, and he wanted Lennie to be no less.

Lennie was angry with him, and letting him know it. He knew her ways, for she was very much like her mother...she carried her chin high when she was mad about something, and kept her eyes fixed straight ahead.

"There's good men around," he said. "I don't want my daughter marrying a gunfighter."

"My mother married one!"

That silenced him, and she knew it would. Her mother had married him, and it had been the making of him. After his rough and wasted life, she had tamed him down without making him less a man; and the few good years, the few happy years of his life had been with her.

Uneasily, Spanyer's thoughts returned to Considine. Grudgingly, he admired the man. Any man to whom Dutch would run second was sure to be quite a man. And the Kiowa, too. The Kiowa had always played a lone hand except for once...the one time when he had been in the outfit that tried to rob the Obaro bank...the Kiowa had been the only survivor of that raid.

Considine did not seem like an outlaw. He had the air of a gentleman, and there was something undefined in his manner that set him apart. Dave Spanyer, who knew men, found himself doing some straight thinking about Considine.

Just the same, the man was an outlaw. And it was unlikely they would ever meet again. Especially, Spanyer reflected grimly, if they went ahead with what they were undoubtedly planning...a strike at the bank in Obaro.

The sun cleared the ridge behind them and lay hot on their backs. On their left, they were approaching a high rocky hogback, its rifts and gullies drifted with fine white sand.

All around them were clumps of bear grass, saltbush, and desert five-spot. Here and there along the washes the ironwood was in bloom, the flowers appearing along with the misty green of the first leaves.

If they could get to California, he was thinking, it would still not be too late to put in a crop.

"Pa?"

Spanyer glanced around, surprised.

"There's a smoke."

He followed her finger. The smoke was rising straight and tall from somewhere beyond that hogback ridge. He watched it break, then break again, shooting up puffs of smoke.

Turning in the saddle, he looked back, and saw behind them another smoke. It was north of their last night's camp.

"We'll eat," he said suddenly. "We may not get a chance later."

He glanced at the point of rocks ahead. There would be a place up there, with some protection. He slid his Winchester from the boot and they rode on toward the rocks.

They kept wide of the rocks until they were past them, and then he swung sharply around and rode up into them. Only when he was sure there was no one there did he motion for Lennie to join him.

He helped her down, thinking of his wife. Then he

41

took the grub bag down. "Ain't much," he said, ashamed of how little there was.

A man with a daughter should have more. He had felt that way with his wife, too, and it had been a long time before he realized that it was him she loved, and she did not care whether he had much or little. The discovery had been a real shock, for he had never thought of himself as a lovable man, and it stirred him so deeply that he was never quite the same afterward. From that day on his devotion to her had been the ruling passion of his life.

But he had never been at ease with Lennie...maybe it was that school she had gone to. He had never been to school, and he could write only a little, and read scarcely more.

He had known little about women, and now with a daughter who had suddenly become a woman he found himself lacking the knowledge he needed. Being a serious man with a profound sense of duty, this lack troubled and worried him.

The idea that a decent woman could actually like being in a man's arms went against all his upbringing. His wife had...but his wife occupied a place in his consciousness that set her apart from all other women, and he could not even consider her as a sample of womanhood. She was different. She was very special.

He found a few sticks of dried-out wood fallen from a dead cedar up on the hill, and a few partly burned sticks left by some previous traveler. In a hollow among the rocks, where they could observe all who approached without themselves being seen, he built a very small fire.

The wood was completely dry and made no smoke, only a faint shimmer of heat in the air. As he worked, his thoughts returned to Considine.

No gunfighter, sheriff, or outlaw is ever completely unknown to others of his kind. The grapevine of trail herd, stagecoach, and saloon conversation allowed each to know all the others. Thus Dave Spanyer had known of Considine for a long time, had known how he wore his gun, how many men he had killed, what sort of man he was.

A few gunfighters, such as the Earps, Hickok, Billy the Kid, John Ringo, and Wes Hardin, because of some accident that drew public attention became better known than many others who were their equal or better. Along the cattle trails the names of Johnny Bull, Joe Phy, Luke Short, Longhair Jim Courtright, Jeff Milton, Dallas Stoudenmire, King Fisher, and Ben Thompson were just as well known.

Bending over his fire, with occasional glances up and down the trail or at the surrounding country, Dave Spanyer considered all that. He knew of Considine in the way he knew of the others, and Considine had a reputation for being a square man, and one who could stand up and trade bullet for bullet. In Spanyer's hard, tight little world this made him a man.

Still, there was only one end to such a life. You died gun in hand or went to prison, and Dave Spanyer was determined that no daughter of his would have anything to do with a gunfighter.

Yet even as he said these things to himself he was thinking that Pete Runyon had been both an outlaw and a gunfighter, and now he was an officer of the law and a respected citizen. Western people were notoriously ready to forgive...they could forgive anything but lies or cowardice.

A kangaroo rat moved nearer, sniffing inquisitively at the coffee smell. Lennie broke off a corner of a biscuit and tossed it to him. The tiny animal made a prodigious leap, all of seven feet, then stopped and looked back. Seeing there was no pursuit, the inquisitive little creature scuttled back, hopped around, and finally, after inspecting the piece of biscuit, it picked it up in its forepaws and ate daintily.

The pause was brief. They moved on, and the sun was

hot; cicadas hummed in the greasewood. They saw the trail where three peccaries had crossed the road. Once a rattler sounded off from the shade of a rock as they rode by. Above them a lone buzzard circled lazily against the vault of the brassy sky.

Spanyer was thinking of the men he had left, knowing how they felt right now. "Well," he said aloud, "good luck to them."

Lennie glanced at him. She had no need to ask of whom he spoke, for she had been thinking of them, too—of Considine at least, and the way the dark hair curled over his forehead.

How quietly he had faced her father, neither asking for nor refusing trouble! Nor had he made any excuses. The only words had been to clear her, the simplest words he could have spoken, and without apology.

"Pa...?"

He looked over at his daughter, aware of the change in her, for she was no longer angry with him.

"Do you think they'll make it?"

He considered that in the slow way he had; considered the town of Obaro, and then he thought about Considine. After a while he commented, "He'll do it if anybody can." He paused briefly. "The trouble is, Kitten, that's only the beginning. After that they chase you, and you run, if you're smart. Maybe you get away that time, but you can't always get away. When a man lifts his hand outside the law, he sets every man's hand against him.

"And you don't make anything. Leaving honesty out of it, you just can't make it that way. Mighty few outlaws ever sit down to figure out how little they make over the years.

"Knew a big-time outlaw once...a man everybody talked about as being smart. Why, that man had spent a third of his grown-up life in prison, had two death sentences hanging over him, and he was living on handouts from other outlaws and folks."

Spanyer narrowed his eyes at the horizon where the heat waves shimmered above the desert.

In the southwest, a smoke was rising....

SIX

Considine looked at his big silver watch. "You boys come into town at twenty minutes to one. I can promise you ten minutes...fifteen maybe."

Hardy shot him a quick glance. "That's a long fight."

"He's a tough man." He grinned at them, a reckless grin they all knew. "And I'd better be."

He eased himself in the saddle. "And no shooting. Only if it is absolutely necessary. Once the shooting starts, you boys will be bucking some of the best shots in the West. I know—I've shot against them in target matches."

He started off, looked back once and saw them wave, and it gave him a turn to realize what he was leading them into...and they were good men. Good men, and tough.

His thoughts turned to Lennie. It was strange, how right something like that could seem when he had only met the girl. It came to him suddenly that he could not remember ever feeling that way about Mary.... Had it simply been that he was young and Mary was the prettiest girl around?

Or was it that he had finally grown up? His father had said something to him once that he had never forgotten. "Folks talk a lot about the maternal feeling in women, but they say nothing about man's need to protect and care for someone; yet the one feeling is as basic as the other."

There could be something to that. When he was a youngster he had believed his father was out of date and didn't know what was going on, but as he grew older he realized it had been he himself who didn't know what it was all about. And now he had nobody to care for, and nobody who cared a thing about him.

He had drifted into crime when it seemed like a prank. The trouble was, it wasn't any prank. When you threaten men or steal their property it no longer is a prank. It's man stuff, and not very good man stuff, either....

Maybe that was why Lennie appealed to him, because she needed somebody. She needed a man and she needed a home. Maybe it was because he wanted to give her the things a woman needs...and no woman was much account without a home or a man, or both. Anything else was unimportant. All the rest was play-acting.

He drew rein when he came near enough to see the town, and there was little enough of it to see. There were three long streets and a few cross streets, and the bank was there on the main street, right in plain sight. The corral at the livery stable was at the other end of town.

If people knew he was in town they would be expecting a fight, and everybody would be excited and ready for it. The first thing was to let them know he was in town, and the second was to make Pete Runyon good and mad. That would not be easy, for Pete was a cool-headed man who thought things out carefully.

Mary, though...he must see Mary. That would make Pete mad if anything would.

The crowd would gather fast, once word of the fight got around. The fight would draw everybody down near the corrals, and probably only one man would be left in the bank. The holdup should take no more than five minutes. It could be a smooth, fast job, and with luck they would be off and away before the fight was over.

If something happened so that guns were fired, then he would lose his crowd fast, and he would have to get out of town the best way he knew how. But what if Pete grew suspicious and started putting two and two together? Then his tail would really be in the crack.

Considine started his horse again. He drew his gun and spun the cylinder, then checked the spare gun he always carried in his saddlebag.

The horse he was riding was strange to him, but Honey Chavez said it was the fastest he had. Their own horses would be waiting for them at the box canyon hideout, so they could run these hard getting away, make a quick switch, and head south on their fresh horses.

The great difficulty, of course, was in these things for which one could not plan successfully—the unexpected, the mistakes made by others which could not be foreseen. A man packing a gun might walk into the bank at the wrong time; somebody might leave the bank and then return; or somebody with a rifle handy might be in one of the second-floor windows.

Runyon might score a lucky punch and knock him cold...or, just as bad, he might knock Runyon out. The fight must last ten minutes at the very least.

He looked off to the west, and saw smoke rising. He swore bitterly, remembering that Spanyer and Lennie were traveling that way.

His thoughts reverted to the problem before him, and he ticked off one by one some of the things he must consider and for which they had tried to plan.

Mrs. O'Beirne, for instance. That woman never missed a thing, and she kept a shotgun handy. She had used it on a bunch of Indians once with terrible effect. She was nobody to take lightly; after the death of her husband she had put on pants and roped and branded her own stock.

Tilting his hat back so his face could be plainly seen, he drew up on the edge of town and rolled a cigarette. His mouth felt dry, and there was a tightness in his stomach. Straightening himself in the saddle, he rode around the end of the corral and into the street.

In his mind he saw the whole vast area around the town as though he soared above it. Here lay the town; to the west rode Spanyer and his daughter. Behind him, soon to turn off in this direction, rode Hardy, Dutch, and the Kiowa. These were the small parts of a machine that had already started to move inexorably toward a given point in time.

He was not on the wanted list in Obaro. It was known that he had robbed those trains long ago, but there had been no evidence. He could ride freely into the town.

Here he had lived. These people he knew. He also knew that if he successfully robbed their bank they would pursue him as far as they could, they would capture or kill him if possible; but secretly they would be pleased that, since it had been done, one of their own boys had done it.

He knew the peculiar philosophy of these people, knew the part that daring and excitement played in their lives. And he knew with a pang that all that was changing.

With watchful eyes he rode into the street; unconsciously he tipped his hat forward again. A few loafers sat on the gallery in front of the Emporium, which was two blocks down the street. Mrs. O'Beirne was sweeping off her steps.

A hen pecked at something in the street, a dog rolled in the warm dust. Several horses were hitched to the rail.

One by one he checked off the things he saw, glancing once, sharply, at the bank from under his hat brim, then he tilted it back on his head once more so they could see his face. He wanted to be recognized...they must all know he was in town.

As he drew abreast of the harness shop he saw a man who was standing inside come suddenly to the door and stare at him. He heard the startled exclamation: "Doc! Did you see what I saw?"

Somewhere a door slammed....

Considine was back in town.

Around the corner just ahead of him was Pete Runyon's house—the house where he lived with Mary. The picket fence had been painted a fresh white, and the small lawn was green and smooth. Climbing roses grew over the porch.

Now people were coming to the doors to look at him, and the loafers in front of the Emporium were all on their feet.

A big man with a blond walrus mustache yelled at him: "Hey, Considine! You back to stay?"

Considine drew rein. "Hiya, Matt! See you're fat as ever."

"We never figured to see you around here."

Considine dropped his cigarette into the street. Had he seen a curtain move in the Runyon window? He grinned easily. "Why, I've got friends in town, Matt. I came back to see Pete Runyon. I hear he's been keeping in shape."

He glanced at the sun. Not much time, and he could not cut it too fine. He turned the corner and dismounted in front of the white gate.

Taking off his hat, he knocked the dust from his jeans. He was jumpy inside...nerves. But some of the old deviltry was rising within him, and for the first time in days he felt genuine anticipation for what lay before him.

Mary had always been too serious, and she would be

too serious now. He looked at the house as he opened the gate. Well, she had what she wanted, and it looked like Mary, too, all neat and precise and pretty.

Mary knew all the little tricks of binding a man tight; she knew exactly what she wanted in her neat, definite little life...well, maybe that was all right for Pete. Suddenly, and for the first time since she had thrown him over for Pete Runyon, Considine felt a vast relief.

He went up on the porch, his spurs jangling. There was a screen door, and the inner door was open. He stepped inside. It was a stuffy little parlor with a Brussels carpet and stiff chairs covered with dark red plush. Each of the chairs had a neat white antimacassar on the back. It was a proud, pretentious little room, stiffly, primly respectable.

The room was Mary, so completely that Considine felt suddenly sorry for Runyon. How much had she changed him?

"Anybody home?"

His voice boomed into the stillness within the house, somehow faintly indecent in that strict, upright silence.

Mary Runyon came suddenly into the room, and stopped abruptly. She was shapely in her neat house dress, her hair drawn smoothly back.

She had a certain assurance and poise that he did not remember, probably something that comes to a woman who is loved—or to one who has caught her man and hog-tied him.

"Hello, Mary."

Her face turned white to the lips, and she smoothed her dress with both hands, running them down over her waist, carefully, slowly. It was a gesture she had when she was upset...he remembered it well.

Mary had always been prim and respectable, and it had always angered her that he had the ability to excite her physically. Considine grinned at the memory of it. She had

51

hated the idea of it, for it offended her sense of the pro-
prieties.

"What do you want?"

Her voice was sharp, without gladness or welcome.
Yes, he thought, this is Mary. She had her man and her
home, and his return was a threat, a danger.

"Where's Pete?"

"He's not here." She gathered her apron in her fingers
and seemed to dry her already dry hands. "What are you
doing here? Why couldn't you stay away?"

"Figured we might talk over old times, Mary." He
grinned at her, a taunting grin. She flushed and grew angry.

"Go away! Leave us alone!"

Considine did not move. This was the worst part. His
eyes went to the clock on the mantel. "I won't be staying,"
he said. "I just came back to see Pete."

"You will see him if you stay. He isn't afraid of you."

"Pete? Pete Runyon was never afraid of anybody or
anything...even when he knew I could beat him with a
gun, he wasn't afraid."

He glanced around the room. "Well, you must really
have him hog-tied or he'd never sit still for a room like this,
Mary." He looked into her eyes. "Better give him some
rope, Mary. You tie a man too tight and he strangles. You
let a man have a little leeway, and if he loves you he will
tie himself, and like it."

"Pete isn't tied down," she protested. "He's a responsible man. He means something in this town." She lifted
her eyes to his again. "What do you mean to anybody?
Anywhere?"

He felt the stab of truth, but brushed it away. Yet it
was true, for he meant nothing, anywhere, to anybody. And
then suddenly he thought of Lennie. Maybe he did mean
something—if only a little—to somebody.

"You're wrong, Mary. I've got a girl of my own."

Her eyes sharpened, and he remembered something

else about Mary. She had never liked to lose anything, even when she didn't want it. Yet, taking her all around, he supposed she was a good woman. She kept a good house, she was attractive-looking, and probably Pete would wind up as mayor, or something.

"She would have to take the guns away from you and turn you into a responsible citizen or you'd be worth nothing to her!"

"Like Pete? You'd probably want her to pin on a star and run my best friend out of town."

"You know Pete didn't want to do that! He had to...after all that happened."

"And to keep you!"

Mary Runyon was furious now. "Get out! Get out of my house! I hope I never see you again!"

He turned on his heel and walked out, and stood there for a moment in the bright sunshine. Well, what had that accomplished? But all he wanted it to accomplish was to make Pete mad enough to fight...and maybe it would.

Yet he felt tight and strange inside, and suddenly he knew the last thing he wanted to do was fight Pete Runyon. In fact, it would be good to see him again...like old times.

How many head of cattle had they branded together? How many times when working for the same cow outfit had they fought off Indians or rustlers? How many head of cattle had they snaked out of bogs? How many saloon brawls had they fought side by side?

He gathered his reins and stepped into the saddle, and suddenly Mary was beside him, grasping at his sleeve. "Considine...I don't care what you think of me, but don't hurt Pete!" She clung to his hand. "Please, leave him alone!"

Astonished, he looked down at her twisted, anguished face. "Why, Mary! You really love him, don't you?"

Suddenly her face was still. "Yes...yes, Considine, I do love him. He's my man."

Well, I'm forever damned, he thought. *This is Mary. Mary, who struggled against every emotion, and whom he used to delight to take into his arms because he knew she responded to something in him, though she fought against it, hating herself for showing it. Even for feeling it.*

"Mary," he said gently, "Pete and I have a little matter to settle, but Pete and I have fought before, and that's all it will be. Maybe he'll whip me again, maybe I'll whip him, but I'll make you one promise, Mary, and it is the only one I can make. I won't draw a gun on him."

He rode off, and she stared after him for an instant, then gathering her skirt, she started to run.

There were several buckboards on the street now, and thirty or forty horses were tied along the hitching rails. More people were on the street than was usual at this hour of the morning, so he knew the word had spread. Under other circumstances, with a fight like this about to come off, he would have been out there himself to watch.

He swung down and tied his horse with a slip knot. He removed his hat and then put it back on, and in the moment of settling it on his head his eyes went toward the bank. Nobody stood in front of it...nobody seemed to be coming or going.

He did not see Mary Runyon run to Mrs. O'Beirne's, where the words rushed from her. "Have you seen Pete? Considine is looking for him!"

Mrs. O'Beirne merely glanced at her. "Now don't worry your head about Pete! He'll know what to do...he'll do what he did before!"

Considine had stopped next door to the office of the sheriff. The clock in the bank window said it was eleven-thirty. He was really sweating it out now. Things had to happen fast...the worst of it was, Pete was a slow man to anger.

54

Somewhere a horseshoe rang against an iron peg. That might be Pete...he was a man who liked to pitch horseshoes, and was good at it.

Suddenly, from the area back of the sheriff's office, he heard Mary's voice. "Pete! Pete, Considine's in town!"

"Is he now?"

"Pete, he wants trouble...I just know he does!" Her voice grew strident. "Pete, don't fight with him! Just put him in jail!"

Pete's laugh was deep, rich, amused. "Now, Mary, you know nobody could put Considine in jail without a fight. What do you expect of me?"

Then Pete Runyon came around the corner of the building and their eyes met. Considine had to fight back an impulse to step up and thrust out his hand. He liked this man. He had always liked him...but he needed that stake, he needed that money in the bank—or did he?

He shook off his doubts, angry with himself. Of course he needed it!

"What do you want, Considine? I take it this isn't a social call?"

"Not unless you think getting your noggin beat off is social."

Men were gathering around, eager not to miss a word, or a blow. Involuntarily, Considine's eyes strayed up the street. He could see a man dismounting from a horse up near the bank. The man was Dutch.

"Did you have to come back?" Pete asked.

"Sure...to push your face into the mud of Jensen's stable yard!"

Mary was behind Pete, and so he added, wanting to get started, "And I want to show your wife how her pretty boy looks with his face all mussed up!"

Pete Runyon flushed, but he was puzzled, trying to grasp what lay behind this. Considine was worried. If Run-

55

yon started thinking...He was canny, and moreover he knew Considine too well...if he had time to think he would figure this out, and there would be hell to pay.

"What's the matter, Pete? Has marriage slowed you down? Don't tell me you're getting fat in the belly as well as the head?"

Runyon's features settled into hard lines. "I never backed out of a fight in my life, and you damned well know it!"

Considine chuckled tauntingly. "Not before you got married. Has she trimmed your horns, Pete?"

Runyon's face darkened angrily. He took half a step forward, his fist cocked.

Considine backed away. "Not here, Pete. Down where we fought before—on the same ground. You were lucky there, and you'd better be lucky this time!"

Considine turned to the crowd. "I'm going to lick your sheriff, unless he's too scared to fight."

Wheeling, he started down the street toward the corral. The clock said eleven-forty.

A man stood in the door of the bank wearing a green eye-shade and sleeve garters. That would be Epperson. Trust Epperson not to miss a good fight.

Considine hung his jacket over his saddle-horn and led his horse off down the street, the crowd following. He could hear Pete arguing with Mary, but he did not stop. It had to work now...it must work.

Turning into Larson's feed lot, he put his horse where he could easily get to it, and faced around to meet Runyon. His mouth was dry and his stomach felt empty.

Watch that right, he warned himself. Watch his right and keep moving. Don't let him get set.

Mrs. O'Beirne stood on her steps talking to Mary. "Now don't you worry your head. I'll not deny it will be a fight, and I've been looking forward to seeing it."

"But Pete..." Mary started to protest.

"A fight never hurt a man, Mary Runyon. Now don't you worry."

Mrs. O'Beirne looked at Considine. "That boy! And he came from such a fine family! I've always said that things would have been different if the Apaches hadn't wiped them out when he was a youngster."

Pete Runyon had taken off his coat and his guns and hung them on the fence. He turned now and moved toward Considine, but he was still puzzled...worried about something.

Considine fixed that. He stepped in quickly and slapped Pete Runyon across the mouth.

Dutch had dismounted in front of the saloon, and he looked like any big, lazy, rather fat man as he walked into the bank, brushing by the banker and the cashier who stood in the door, looking toward the corral. Not a man was in sight this side of the corral, anywhere along the street.

Dutch pulled out a twenty-dollar gold piece. "I'd like some change for this, mister."

Reluctantly, the cashier turned from the door and walked back into the bank. Two riders on dusty horses drew up before the bank just then and one of them got down. Through the window Dutch saw Hardy starting for the door.

The banker turned from the door. "Damn it, if I wasn't a businessman, I'd—"

Hardy put the gun in his back just as Dutch produced his gun on the startled cashier. Leaving both men to be guarded by Hardy, Dutch went behind the wicket, avoiding the glass door.

With swift, practiced movements, he picked up the neat stacks of eagles and swept the gold into his sack. From down the street came the sound of shouts and wild cheering.

There was no waste motion, no hesitation. As swiftly

57

as he had stripped the counters and safe of the gold, Dutch came around the counter, put down the sack, and bound and gagged the banker and the cashier. Then he picked up the sack and the two men went out into the street, where the Kiowa waited.

"Dutch," Hardy said, "I'd sure like to see that fight!"

"So would I. Come on!"

They walked their horses for the first block, turned down the chosen alley and trotted through the dust, then turned into the hills, and began to ride swiftly.

Once, topping out on a ridge, they looked back. There was no pursuit.

"I hope he makes it," Hardy said. "I surely hope he does!"

"He'll make it."

The Kiowa said nothing at all. He liked the weight of the sack he was carrying, and he was already thinking of Mexico.

Dutch indicated a far ridge. "Smoke," he said. "We'll need all the breaks we can get to reach the border."

By rights Considine should be leaving town about now. He had the fastest horse and should catch them.

On the rim of the distant ridge the smoke lifted a questioning finger, and somewhere farther toward the west another replied.

Dark-skinned warriors riding their shaggy ponies came down out of the draws of that distant ridge like hawks sailing from the high rocks and they scattered in a ragged rank, heading toward the west.

The finger of smoke talked of two people riding one horse...it would be easy, almost too easy.

Their faces were wide across the cheekbones and dark, their eyes like slits of obsidian. Knees clutching the lean flanks of their horses, they rode west.

SEVEN

That slap across the mouth had just the effect Considine had known it would, for nothing is so calculated as to drive a man to fury.

Whatever had been worrying Runyon was gone. He moved in swiftly, his fists cocked. Considine watched him coming, and stabbed suddenly with a left that caught Runyon coming in. It was a jarring blow, but Pete kept coming, and ducking suddenly he swung a high overhand right.

Considine saw it coming, but it was fast, faster than any such punch had a right to be. It caught Considine on the side of the head and staggered him. The crowd yelled, and the two men went into each other slugging.

Considine's foot rolled on a stone and he reeled. Runyon caught him with a wicked left that exploded lights in Considine's brain, and he tried to clinch, but Runyon moved carefully around, and swung a hard right to the stomach.

59

Considine clinched, and quicker with his feet than Pete, he back-heeled him into the dust, then stepped back with an elaborate show of courtesy to allow him to rise.

Runyon looked up, partly stunned, wholly surprised, for he knew that Considine was nothing if not a good finisher.

He got up, taking his time, puzzled by Considine's neglect. He had seen his former partner fight more than once, and when a man was down he rarely got the chance to get up more than halfway before he was clobbered.

There was an angry welt on Runyon's cheekbone, a cut that trickled blood at the corner of his mouth. He was cautious now, and more dangerous. He would be using his head…and Pete Runyon was a dangerous man. He was two inches over six feet, the same height as Considine, but he was fifteen pounds heavier than Considine's lean one hundred and eight-five.

Pete moved in swiftly, feinted, and swung a right to the neck, then stepped in with a smashing left. They fought toe to toe, slugging, smashing, driving. Pete landed a left to the jaw, then a right. He bored in, ducking his head, then charging and swinging overhand blows with both hands. Considine backed up, tasting blood from a smashing blow on the mouth.

With that taste of blood, he was mad for the first time. He pushed his left hand against Pete's head, then brought up a short right uppercut that lifted Pete's head where a left swing caught him and knocked him staggering into the crowd.

Considine stepped back, gasping for breath. How much time had passed? Half a minute? A minute?

Runyon moved in and swung a left. Grasping the left wrist, Considine pivoted suddenly and threw him over his shoulder, but Pete had fought Considine before and as soon as the move started he went with it, and landed rolling.

On his feet again, Runyon moved in, and again the two men slugged until they were streaming with sweat and every man and woman in the crowd was hoarse from shouting. Pete caught Considine with a right and knocked him down.

Considine hit the ground hard, shaken by the fall, and he rolled over, starting to get up. *Time? How much time?*

He took his time getting up, wiped the dust from his hands, and walked in. He stabbed a left to Runyon's mouth and was rushed to the corral fence, where he brought up with a crash. He slipped out of the corner, hit Pete again, and a right grazed his own jaw.

They rushed together, clinched, and Pete back-heeled Considine to the ground. He fell, but he got his feet under him and took a breath while the crowd shouted for him to rise.

Considine's head was buzzing…the roaring of the crowd and the roaring in his skull seemed one and the same. He got up, and Pete charged him. Considine met him with a right to the jaw that smashed Runyon full length on the ground.

Pete lay still, felled like an ox under the slaughterer's axe.

Panic flooded Considine. If Pete was out…he could visualize the crowd flooding back up the street at the moment his men emerged from the bank.

Gasping and bloody, he moved forward, and in that instant Pete Runyon got up.

Lying face down, he shoved up suddenly and drove at Considine's knees. Considine came down with a thud and they rolled over and over on the ground, fighting and gouging while the crowd roared. Breaking free, they came up together and fell to slugging with a will. Suddenly, all animosity was gone and both men were filled with the sheer joy of combat. Slugging toe to toe, they moved back and forth across the dusty corral, slamming away exuberantly with both hands.

Runyon was grinning now and, in spite of himself, so

was Considine. All his struggle to make it look like a grudge battle was gone. He liked this big man he was fighting, and there was no beating around the bush. He ducked a right fist and smashed his right into Runyon's belly. Runyon grunted, sagged at the knees, then clinched and butted him under the chin with his head.

Considine's teeth clicked together and he fell back onto the ground. When he got up he felt a right smash his lips. He spat blood into the dust and heard a great roaring in his head. He feinted and dropped Pete to his knees with a right fist.

Pete got up slowly. He doubled his big fists and bored in, and they fought gasping for breath, wrestling, grunting with the force of the blows, and smashing wickedly at each other.

Considine was exhausted. He did not know how Pete felt, but he knew that he was all in. Pete was a bruiser, no question about it. Considine feinted, slammed a right to the wind, and tried the same combination again and was dropped to his knees when Pete countered swiftly.

How much time? How long had they been fighting?

His feet felt heavy and his arms were tired. He moved in—and suddenly a whip cracked. He saw Mary beside them, and she held a whip and was drawing it back. Only his suddenly up-thrown arm saved him from serious injury.

"Pete, you stop this! Stop it now, or I'll leave this town and I'll leave you!"

Pete turned to protest and Considine brushed a hand across his bloody face. "What's the matter, Pete? Quitting?"

Mary turned on him, but before she could speak men moved between them. "Better ride, Considine—you've had your fight. I'd say it was even up."

Considine looked over their heads at Runyon, and found again that puzzled expression on his face.

Considine lifted a hand. "It was a good fight, Pete! Good-bye...and *thanks!*"

He missed the stirrup with his foot the first time, then made it. *Not too fast now*, he warned himself.

As he rode past the bank he saw a sign hung on the closed door: OUT TO LUNCH.

That would hold them all but Epperson. He would come back to the bank—but he might stop and talk about the fight for a while.

His head ached and his jaw was stiff. He spat blood into the dust and swore, and even the swearing hurt. That damned Pete always could punch. Luckily, his hands were in good shape...they were puffed and swollen, but unbroken. His hands had always been good, they were powerful hands, square across the knuckles and strong. Now he worked his fingers to keep the stiffness from them.

The last buildings of the town fell behind, and he lifted the horse into a trot, then a canter. When he was out of sight of town he ran the horse for half a mile, then slowed to a canter again. Twice he looked back from ridges, but saw no pursuit.

It had gone well, almost too well, yet he felt no elation. What had he done, after all, but thumb his nose at a lot of people who had everything he did not? He always said he had his freedom, but what sort of freedom is it when every sheriff may be hunting for you?

He let the horse canter for a short distance, then ran it again. He saw Dutch before he reached the canyon, for Dutch was standing out there watching for him. In some ways Dutch was like an old mother hen. Considine swung to the ground, and Hardy moved in quickly and switched his saddle to his own horse for him.

Dutch stared at Considine's face. "How was it?"

Considine merely looked at him and said, "I told you he could punch."

They stepped into their saddles and started out. The route had been carefully scouted beforehand and they knew what they had to do. The horses had been freed, and

63

they would eventually drift back to Honey's place or to the ranches from which he had gotten them.

Riding through the soft sand of the wash, they mounted a steep bank and cut across the top of the mesa.

"Saw a smoke a while back," Hardy said. Hardy was young. He always had something to say.

"We'll see a lot of them."

Considine was tired, but his weariness was as much mental as physical. They had brought it off—up to a point. Now they had to get away.

He glanced back at their trail. Nothing in sight. By now they knew. By now Pete Runyon realized what the fight was all about, and he would be good and mad. So would the rest of them be mad...and although some of them would think it a good joke, it would not keep them from running him down and shooting him if he made a fight of it.

His face throbbed with every step of his horse. It was puffed and bruised and cut. Sweat trickled into the cuts, but the sting and smart of the cuts was nothing to the memory of the part he had played back there. Granted that outlaws would be talking of it for years...what had he done?

It was Dutch who first saw the smoke. "Now what could that be?" he said, pointing toward the billowing cloud rising ahead of them.

"I hope it ain't what it looks to be," Hardy commented. "I left my girl's picture in that store."

Slowing their pace, each man shucked his rifle from its scabbard. Considine swung wide on the flank and a little in advance. The Kiowa fell back, on the far side. They came up to the store at a fast walk, a line of mounted skirmishers.

The store was gone...only the adobe walls of one building remained, probably just as Honey Chavez had found it, long ago.

"Tracks," Hardy said, indicating them. "Fire still burning. They can't be gone very long."

"He kill," the Kiowa pointed to a large patch of blood. "Chavez kill this one."

Considine rode quickly around. The Indians were gone...all their dead and wounded carried off, as usual.

"He made a fight of it," Hardy said. "I'd never have believed he had it in him. He must have killed three, by the look of things. Wounded a couple."

Although they saw Chavez' body lying there, they could not take time to bury him, but Chavez would have been the first to understand that. Let the posse do it.

They rode out swiftly. There was nothing to keep them now. Westward at first, then south into the desert and toward the border.

They went down the trail at a canter, all of them seeing the tracks of the Indian ponies in the dirt, superimposed upon the tracks of Lennie and her father. The Apaches would have seen those tracks, and they would know one of the riders was a woman...a good tracker would know which horse she rode.

By this time Dave Spanyer would know what was behind him and the man was no tenderfoot. He had been up the mountain and over the hill, and he knew a lot about trouble and the packages in which it presented itself. And from what Dutch said the old man had told him, Lennie could handle her rifle better than most men.

It was very hot. The air was still. They rode at a good pace, conserving the strength of their horses, yet keeping up a steady, distance-eating gait.

The original plan was still good: to strike into the very heart of the desert, keeping to the *tinajas* and seeps, the water holes least frequented by the Indians and incapable of supplying more than four or five men at a time.

The sky was a vast emptiness. Considine gave no thought to the money in the sacks they carried. He was thinking of the girl on the trail, and her father...and some-where between them, the Apaches.

Hours earlier, Dave Spanyer had come to his moment of bleak decision.

Before that, he had done a lot of soul-searching. Irritably, he ran over in his mind the events of the night before. After all, when a girl got to Lennie's age she had to be trusted. What if something happened to him? She would be on her own, anyway, and the only way she would learn about men was by meeting them...besides, every bit of trail-side rumor he had heard said that Considine was a gentleman.

"I ain't much of a father," he said suddenly. "Never had much truck with women folks. Never rightly understood them. Your Ma was different. She knew how to handle me, but I just do the wrong things, Lennie. You got to make allowances."

She said nothing, so he searched for words as they rode through the hot, still afternoon. "Had your Ma lived we'd have made out, and she'd want you to marry a good man and have a home, and that's what I want for you."

It was only a few hours ago that the rain had ceased, yet there was small indication of it except for some cracked mud in the bottom of a hollow here and there. But his instinct told him that water would be the least of their troubles before this ride was over. He wiped his rifle free of dust, then bit off a chew of tobacco.

He scanned the desert and the mountains. A man never knew there were Apaches around until they started to shoot—not unless he kept his eyes open.

But his thoughts kept reverting to Lennie. He wanted to reach her, to make her understand. He groped for words, yet every trail his thoughts tried to follow led into an unfamiliar jungle of ideas where he was not at home.

Finally he said, "There's more to loving a man than kissing and such."

"I know there is, Pa."

Relieved at her response, he went on, "Next shade, we'll pull up for a bit."

They must keep their horses fresh, for there was no telling when they might have to run for it.

Suddenly, in front of them, they saw the tracks that came out of the desert to the southeast and cut across their trail. Six unshod ponies, the tracks not an hour old....

Spanyer studied their trail, looked off in the direction toward which they were riding, but saw nothing. "Might have seen us," he said. "We'd better take care."

"Pa?"

"Huh?"

"About them...Considine and the others. Do you think they made it?"

"No tellin'."

"Will they come this way?"

"They'll light out fast for Mexico. From what I hear tell, that Considine knows the desert like an Apache or a Pima."

"I liked him."

"You just forget him. You'll likely never see him again, but if he comes gallivantin' around you, I'll kill him."

Spanyer turned in the saddle to look behind him, but the desert was empty...he saw no dust. Yet worry lay heavy upon him, and he could not ride easy. He kept twisting and turning, and he knew the symptoms—he only felt like this when he had the feeling of being watched.

He could see nothing, but he knew they were in trouble now, and he did not need to see it. Those tracks were too fresh...trust an Indian to see them. So what to do?

Dave Spanyer had no illusions about the situation. Once you had Apaches on your trail you were in trouble...all kinds of trouble. They would attack...they would probably try an ambush, to kill him. Yet they might not.

Suppose Considine and his bunch had gotten away? They would be coming this way, and if he waited...but he decided against it. The chance of their escaping scot-free was too slight for him to rest any hopes on it. The best thing was to keep going...and it might be he could find a place where he could make a stand.

"Pa...how did you meet my mother?"

Preoccupied as he was with Apaches, the question startled him.

"Oh...she came west with her husband, and he took a fever and died. Being around, I sort of stopped by, time to time, to see if she was making out.

"Your Ma was a real lady...educated...she made me promise to see that you got some schooling.

"I never did figure out what she saw in me. Them days I was younger, and maybe not so mean, but anyway I respected her more than anybody I ever knew. We had a good life, a good life."

His eyes had not ceased to move as he talked, nor had he missed anything. Now he said, very quietly, "Lennie, you slip that Winchester out of its scabbard. Easy now...and be ready for trouble."

"Are they Indians, Pa?"

Her horse was a half-broken mustang, and the rattler was almost under its feet. At the sound of the rattle, the mustang leaped into the air and came down running.

The horse lunged into the rocks, then broke loose on a dead run. Rounding a huge boulder, it hit the top of the rock slide running, and had no chance. The rock started to move under its hoofs, and the horse struggled madly to keep its feet, then fell and rolled over amid a cascade of rocks.

Cursing wildly, Spanyer plunged his own horse in

pursuit, even as he heard the crash of the falling rock and his daughter's scream.

Swinging around the rocks, he drew up and slid to the ground, yet even now he took a quick glance around—this was no time to be off the trail. He half ran, half slid down the rocks to Lennie's side.

She was already getting up. She was shaken, and undoubtedly bruised and skinned, but there seemed to be no broken bones. And she had clung to her rifle. He went past her to the horse.

Even before he reached it he could see that its leg was broken. There was no hope for it—the leg was badly shattered, and for all he knew it had a snake bite too. He stripped off the pack behind the cantle of the saddle, then, not wishing to risk a shot, he stooped quickly and with his Bowie knife cut the horse's throat.

Lennie started toward him and he stopped her. "Gone," he said brusquely, to cover his fear. "Leg broken. I had to kill him."

"Oh, Pa!" Tears started in her eyes. "He was such a fine horse!"

"Are you crazy? That was a rattle-brained, hammer-headed broom-tail, and never an ounce of good to anybody." He paused. "Nevertheless, we're going to miss him."

One horse between them now, and hundreds of miles to go, most of it desert.

"We'll make out with one horse," he said when they got to the top of the slide. "You mount up."

She squinted into the shimmering heat. She knew what was troubling her father, but there was nothing she could do. Without her, he might have had a chance.

Oddly enough, although the Apaches worried him, he thought of them as a present and certain danger which he understood; what disturbed him more was the fact that

69

Lennie needed him so badly, or needed somebody, and he did not know what to do.

Walking ahead of the horse, he plodded steadily into the hot, dead air of the afternoon desert.

EIGHT

Dave Spanyer had never known a time when he did not possess a gun, and use it when needed. The frontier where he grew up made guns a necessity, for despite what some easterners thought about the Indians, the Indian was first and last a warrior.

His standards of behavior had nothing to do with the standards of the white men who opposed him, nor was he properly understood except by a very few people—and all of them were men who had lived with and around Indians.

Failure to understand Indian standards and ideas had done as much harm as had well-meaning but uninformed people, do-gooders and such, and the political appointees who were the Indian agents.

One of the basic mistakes in dealing with people of another cultural background is to attribute to them the ideas one has oneself. For instance, the white man's standards of what constitutes mercy are strictly his own, and the

71

American Indian had no such ideas. Battle was his joy. Battle and horse-stealing, combined with hunting, were his only means to honor and wealth, and a good horse thief was honored and respected more than a good hunter. An Indian would go miles upon miles to steal horses or get into a good fight.

Dave Spanyer had never known a time when he was not in the vicinity of Indians, usually hostile ones. He understood them, often hunted with them, fought them when necessary. He knew that for an Apache the word cruelty had no meaning. Torture was amusing to him, and he felt no sympathy for a captured enemy. The Apache respected courage, fortitude, and strength, for these were qualities by which he himself survived. He also respected cunning.

On the whole, Dave Spanyer had more respect for most Indians than for many of the white men he had known. He fought them, and they fought him, but each respected the other.

The Indians understood and fought each other, and their customs and occupations were much the same until the white man entered the scene with superior weapons, a different set of standards, and a persistence scarcely understood by the Indian, who fought his battles for sport, for honor, and for loot, but rarely for territory to be seized and held.

Choosing the ground for a fight was not easy to do when the Apache was the enemy, for he knew every inch of his desert land, and was a master in the use of terrain from a tactical sense. Dave Spanyer, however, knew this country south of the Gila and the Salt River Valley almost as well as did any Apache.

He had no doubt they had followed every step of his progress for some time, and by now they had decided where the fight was to take place. By this time they undoubtedly knew something of him, too, for a man on a trail in Indian country soon reveals himself to a skilled observer. He reveals himself in the way he travels, in his approach to possible ambuscades, in his use of terrain for ease of travel and for concealment, in his observation of tracks and the country around.

Dave Spanyer wanted to get into a position where an attack must come...where he could get in the first shot, carefully aimed. It was easier to kill that first man...when the firing became more general, men became careful.

Night was not far off. If they could find an easily defended position they might hold off the Apaches until darkness, and escape during the night.

Packsaddle Mountain lay to the south, and the cave at Castle Dome was beyond reach. Then he thought of the canyon on High Lonesome. There was a lot of rocky surface there, and it was a place where they might lose their pursuers.

This was farther west than the Apache usually came, for the Papogoes and Pimas to the south and east were his deadly enemies, and there were Yumas to the south and Mohaves to the north.

Spanyer glanced at the sun. Two hours, at least, until sundown.

"We'll go to High Lonesome," he said aloud.

"Pa?"

"Huh?"

"That Considine...is he a bad man?"

Dave Spanyer studied the question with care. His first impulse was to tell her that he was, and then, thinking of the Apaches, he decided that whatever she might have to dream on would be a help. Besides, as men go, Considine was better than most.

Spanyer knew that no man could be judged except against the background of his time. The customs and moral standards of a time were applicable only to that time, and Considine was a man who left big tracks. He was an outlaw, but so far as Spanyer knew he had been honorable, except in looting stages and, rarely, banks or trains.

"No," he said at last, "I reckon he's not. He's an outlaw, but he's got the makin's of a mighty good man."

And then, strangely, Lennie touched his arm with her fingers, and for a time she walked beside him for a little way, holding his arm. And Spanyer, who had known little of tenderness, and who had found only mystery in the sudden growing up of his daughter, was deeply moved.

Around them the desert changed. The dead-white and faint buff of the sands became deeper in tone, the rocks were darker, and here and there ancient fingers of lava pushed down from the mountains, thrusting their probing fingers into the sand.

Joshua trees lifted their contorted arms toward the empty skies as though caught and petrified in some agonized writhing. On their right was an inclined shelf of almost smooth rock, half a mile long and reaching upwards, unbroken for several hundred feet—a great upthrust, honed and smoothed by wind and rain and sand.

He was reaching back into his memory now. Before High Lonesome Canyon there was a box canyon. That could be the trap...it was an ideal place for an attack, a place to be skirted widely.

Spanyer turned abruptly at right angles away from the mountains, and out into the tumbled forest of boulders. When well among the boulders he turned westward again.

"A man like Considine," Spanyer said suddenly, "is apt to be heedless of discipline, and every man needs discipline. If it isn't given to him, he had better discipline himself. Somewhere Considine took a wrong turn, and it is up to him to take a right one. But he has to do it himself."

"You did."

"Without your Ma...well, without her maybe I'd never have done it."

"Considine could do it." She spoke with confidence.

"A man needs a push sometimes. He needs something outside of himself."

"Pa...the gray's limping."

Dave Spanyer felt the cold hand of death touch him. He turned, almost afraid to look, and led the horse forward, watching it. The gray was limping, all right.

He stopped briefly in the shade of a boulder and examined the hoof. The shoe was broken, and half of it had fallen away. He pried the other half loose, and then with his knife he pared the hoof flat.

They moved on, dipping into a forest of Joshua trees. The sun was very hot, glaring into their faces, bathing them in impossible heat. Nothing moved. Not a dust devil...not a wisp of grass...nothing.

Then suddenly a rabbit plunged into the trail, saw them, and veered sharply off.

Instantly, Spanyer drew his gun and moved back into the rocks. He pressed Lennie down, drew the horse into shelter. He listened into the stillness and it gave back no sound. Holstering his pistol, he shifted his rifle to his right hand from the saddle scabbard.

"Something up there," he said. "A rabbit don't jump like that in this heat unless he's scared."

He squatted on his heels, his Winchester ready. He eased back the hammer, almost to full cock, then, grinding his heel into the sand to stifle the sound, to full cock.

He started to turn his head when he heard the scrape of moccasins on rock. He turned swiftly on the ball of his right foot, slamming his back against the rocks just as the Indian sprang.

The Winchester leaped in Spanyer's hand, and the Apache's throat vanished in a red smear as the bullet tore through, ripping the neck wide.

The sound of the shot slapped against the rock walls, then echoed away and lost itself among the distant sands.

Lennie shrank from the body, which had fallen within

75

reach of them. He had been young, this Apache, and over-eager—and the chance-takers never last.

Silence followed....Were there others near? Or had this one raced on ahead?

The Indian had carried a Winchester and had a Mexican bandolier filled with cartridges. Spanyer shucked these from their loops one by one and filled his pockets. The Winchester was old. He took it in his hands and smashed it against a boulder, then threw it aside.

Lennie glanced at the Indian. "He looks very young," she whispered.

"Old as he'll ever be," Spanyer said dryly.

Dave Spanyer knew patience. Somewhere out there were enemies, so for the time he would not move. He settled back, trying to think his way out.

The horse must be saved. Food and water and a fresh shoe would put it in shape again, and they would need the horse when they got where they were going. And if they took a route out past that basaltic rock they would be in the sand, where their steps would make no sound.

Only a mile farther and the entrance to High Lonesome began. It was no sanctuary, for there was no such place with Indians around, but it was a better place to make a stand. There was water, and they would be on familiar ground.

He plotted every move they must make, once darkness came, and then he set back and rolled a smoke. Having done all that a man could do, he waited.

The rest would do them good...tomorrow would be a long, long day.

At sundown, when the first shadows moved out from the cliff walls, Considine found the horse with its broken leg and cut throat. He drew rein, and the others came up and ranged alongside in a ragged line, looking down upon the dead animal.

The scene required no explanation. It told its own grim story, perhaps the prelude to one even more stark; for without a horse, in desert country, with Apaches on their trail, they would have small chance. This was no country in which to ride double, even if there were no Indians.

Whatever a man does leaves a trail behind, and in his passing he leaves indications of the manner of man he is, of his character, and even something of his plans. It requires only the observant and understanding eye to read what the trail can show.

Nor does any person stand completely alone in this world, for when he passes he brushes, perhaps ever so slightly, upon others, and each is never quite the same thereafter. The passing of Lennie Spanyer had left no light touch upon the consciousness of the man called Considine.

The four men, loaded with the loot of their robbery, looked upon that dead horse and upon those tracks, and for each there was some personal message. Each was disturbed, but these were men without words, unused to voicing their thoughts for all to hear. Nor had they quite shaped those thoughts into words they could share with each other.

Each of these men was worried, for in those moments in the store each had found that Lennie was in some part his own.

For a brief instant her freshness, her brightness, and her open charm had brought something to them that had not been there before, and left a mark upon them. The danger to Lennie was a danger they all felt.

Nor were they free of the images their own minds held of themselves. The man on horseback, the lone-riding man, the lone-thinking man, possessed an image of himself that was in part his own, in part a piece of all the dime novels he had read, for no man is free of the image his literature imposes upon him.

And the dime novel made the western hero a knight-errant, a man on horseback rescuing the weak and helpless.

Never consciously in their thoughts, to these men without words the image was there—and more. For Lennie was the sweetheart, the sister, the wife, each one of them would have...if only in daytime dreams.

"That's the girl's horse."

Dutch cleared his throat uneasily. "No time to waste. We'd better push on."

They pushed on...and the tracks of the led horse lay in the dust before them.

Spanyer, each man was thinking, was shrewd. Trust him to know what to do...else Lennie's dark hair would hang in some wickiup.

"None of our business," Hardy said brusquely. "I'm a-worryin' to see that Mex gal down Sonora way."

"It isn't far to that *tinaja* in the Pedregosas," Considine said; "let's get along."

When they made that turn toward the *tinaja* they left this trail behind, they left Lennie and Dave Spanyer behind, and they turned south into the desert that lay between them and the Mexican border.

They saw one last smoke before the sun went down, a smoke that ascended straight and unbroken, and then broke twice sharply and clearly. It gave them something to remember during the dark hours of the coming night.

Darkness comes suddenly to the desert, where twilight is quickly gone. A bat dipped and fluttered above them, a star appeared...the serrated ridges gnawed at the deep, deep blue of the evening sky. A far-off coyote spoke the moon, and the hoofs of their horses, the creaking of their saddles, made the only other sounds.

Hardy could contain himself no longer. "It must come to sixty thousand. Sixty thousand in gold!"

There was no response. They were four belted men riding for the border, four men who had chosen to live by the gun...and some day to die by it. One was a man who wanted a woman in Mexico; one was a man who wanted a long, quiet drunk; and there was an Indian who wanted nothing at all. And there was one man who did not know what he wanted.

Only he was beginning to be afraid that he did know.

The Kiowa drew up suddenly. "Dust," he said. "Horses pass."

They waited, a tight knot of men, sitting still in the leather, listening.

The tracks of the Spanyers were hours old, and no other white man would be riding in this country now. So it had to be Indians...and they would be camping somewhere close by.

"A big party...a war party."

"Now how do you know that?" Hardy demanded.

"By the smell." The Kiowa spoke softly. "The paint smell...the medicine smell."

They still waited...listening. One of their horses stamped impatiently. With darkness the desert had become cool. In the thin, clear air of the desert, with no vegetation or water to hold the heat, it is quickly gone.

At last they moved out, and when they stopped, hours later, it was in a nest of boulders where a defense could be made. The way they must go on the morrow was a way that must be watched with care. The *tinajas* where water could be had were few, and to miss one might well be fatal.

They lighted no fire. Nor did they make any sound but the faint whisperings of their clothing as they moved. No boots were removed tonight, only gun belts and hats, and the gun belts and saddle guns were kept close at hand.

Overhead there were many stars. The Kiowa was restless. Finally he spoke very quietly. "Woodsmoke...they are very near."

No comment was made. Considine remembered two men he had found, suspended head down over fires that

79

had cooked them until their skulls burst...and Dutch thought of something he had once seen: a man staked out near an ant hill, up to his chin.

The smoke might come from a fire a hundred yards off—but it was more likely to be half a mile away.

Considine was tired, but not sleepy. "You rest," he told them. "I'll stand watch."

He wrapped his blanket about his shoulders and sat against a boulder, a huge rock that leaned over their small camp. The night was cool, but pleasant. Somewhere nearby someone had broken a branch of *thamnosma*. He could smell the pungent, peculiar odor of the Indian witch-plant.

Under the shelter of his blanket he lighted a cigarette, cupping its tiny red eye in his palm, liking the dry, hot taste of the tobacco. The horses cropped grass, a comforting sound...there was the smell of the horses, of the *thamnosma*, and the stale smell of his own unwashed clothing. That he would change when he got to Mexico. There was little time for washing clothes on the trail.

Why should his thoughts turn to Lennie now? What had there been about that slim, tanned girl in her proud dress, faded from many washings? Had it been the feel of her young body through the thin slip? Or the memory of her cool lips? Or was it something deeper? Was it some response from deep within himself, some response of his own loneliness to the loneliness in her?

He was no thinker, and he had no answers. He drew deep on the cigarette and snubbed it out in the sand. He got up and went among the horses, then he moved beyond the rocks, where he stood listening to the night. There was no sound.

As it was growing gray in the east he shook Dutch awake. The big man got up silently, and Considine then stretched out and slept.

When he was awakened scarcely an hour later, Dutch was making coffee over a tiny, smokeless fire. Hardy was saddling his horse, and the Kiowa had slipped away some-where before daylight. Considine saddled his own horse and that of the Kiowa, then went to the fire for coffee.

The Kiowa returned, coming in among the boulders, and squatted by the fire. "Fourteen...they have fresh scalps."

They looked at him, afraid to ask the question that was in all their minds.

"No long hair...no woman."

The Kiowa drew on a cigarette, and gulped coffee. "They are gone now, but they follow a trail. They expect more scalps today."

"Dave's no fool," Dutch said. "He'll know those In-dians are trailing him."

"That Pete Runyon," Hardy said, "he'll be right be-hind us. We'd better light a shuck."

The desert morning opened around them, bright and amazingly clear. The rocks stood out in sharp relief, the distant mountains seemed close by, and only the solemn finger of beckoning smoke touched an ominous note.

But the smoke, like their hard-hewn faces and the smell of smoke and sweat, was of the desert....

NINE

When it was quite dark, Dave Spanyer took up the lead rope and started out from among the rocks. He had discarded the saddle, for it was more weight than it was worth, and he could come back for it later, if such an opportunity developed.

When the bulk of Packsaddle Mountain was behind them, he turned left into the velvety darkness. He could see only a little, but it was light enough to keep from stumbling over rocks or blundering into cactus. The mountains before them were a black wall offering no identifying features.

Lennie walked beside him, and when possible they kept to the soft sand. When passing through occasional patches of desert brush they carefully held the branches aside so they would not brush against their clothing, a sound easily heard and recognized in the desert night.

At last the sudden dampness told them they faced the canyon, for cool air usually came down those canyons, and to a knowing man it was an indication. Once within the canyon, they were engulfed in a vaster, deeper darkness, for the walls rose five hundred feet above them.

The sand was firm from recent floods following the rain, and it made walking easier, but it would leave tracks.

Spanyer blessed his luck in having a daughter who did not complain. Lennie was a girl to make a mother of men, not weak, sniveling mama's boys. She was a good walker, too, and better than the average man with a rifle.

When they had come two miles into the canyon, they stopped to rest. It would be nearly morning now, although still night-dark in the canyon. Since their start they had come six or seven miles.

"Used to be a shanty up there"—he gestured to the mountains ahead, and spoke in a whisper—"and a cave. It was a hide-out some of the boys used. There's a spring."

Something scurried in the darkness. The horse shifted his feet. Suddenly something bounded in the night, sticks cracked, the brush whispered. The horse jerked up its head at the sounds. Spanyer kept an iron grip on the lead rope, and after a minute the horse quieted.

"Lion," Spanyer explained. "Probably smelled the horse before he smelled us."

The stars kept their shy lamps alight in these last hours of darkness. The canyon narrowed and the walls seemed higher; but they had begun to climb, and after a while the canyon widened out and they found themselves in a small basin. Knee-high grass grew around them, and they could smell the freshness of water.

"We'll rest," said Spanyer. "Come daybreak, I'll get my bearings."

Lennie sat down and cradled her head in her arms, which rested on her knees. She thought of the tall rider with the easy walk—more like that of a woodsman than a cowhand. She could imagine him cutting wood for the fire while she fixed dinner, or washing in a tin basin with his sleeves rolled up over muscular arms, his hair splashed with water and sparkling where the drops caught the sun.

He did not seem like an outlaw—and her own father had changed when her mother married him. Maybe he would come west.... When they got to California she would look around for another place, close to Pa's....

She knew she was dreaming. She knew she would not see him again. For all she knew, he might even now be dead, his body propped up to be photographed, the way they often did with dead outlaws. Or he might be in prison.

Yet she could not admit either possibility, for she knew, deep down within her, that she loved him, and only him. She knew, too, that she was not cut out to be an outlaw's woman. Oh, she could stand the hard travel, the rough living and all... she had done that with Pa ever since leaving school; but she knew what she wanted—a home, a nice ranch with cattle feeding on the hills, a stream somewhere close by, shade trees, and the flowers she would plant.

"We'll move now," her father said. "I can make out the shape of things."

He was an exciting man...she blushed with the memory of how she had felt in his arms...but what must he think of her? Scarcely dressed, and soaked to the skin like that.

They moved on, and the climbing was steady now. In some places it was difficult for the horse, and Lennie found herself gasping for breath. How her father made it she could not imagine, but he seemed made of rawhide and steel wire, for all the effect. At last they reached a cluster of rocks among which there was a spring, partly shaded by mesquite, cottonwood, and willow. From the edge of the rocks one could see all around.

They had come out on top of the canyon, and it lay

like a tremendous gash in the mountain, falling away steeply into its own darkness below them.

"They may not find us," Spanyer said. He glanced at her. "I got to sleep, Lennie. Can you stay awake?"

She did not want to sleep. She wanted to stay awake and think. The Apaches seemed farther away, more unreal than Considine...what was his first name? Oddly enough, she had never heard him called anything but Considine. She knew the memory of him would fade out...it would grow dim and she would forget, and she did not want to forget, for it was the only memory she wished to hold close.

There was so little else. She had been abysmally unhappy at school, although she was a good student. She could remember faintly her mother, a slender, lovely woman who had been tender and thoughtful, but Lennie had been at a friend's when her mother died...only vague impressions remained.

Pa was brusque, often stern, and she knew he was worried about her. Pa was a man who was sure in most things. He handled horses and cattle with easy confidence, and among men he walked his own way, never going around anybody. She knew he was respected...even feared.

Back in Socorro where they had lived for a time she had been surprised to hear the respect with which he was addressed by men like the banker, the sheriff, and the big cattlemen around. He was beholden to no man, and the gun that rode his hip was a known thing. Yet it was not the gun that counted; it was the fact that Pa respected himself.

Those cold eyes of his could chill men...she had heard them say it. Yet in his own rough way he was a good father, and a kind one, even though he often said and did the wrong thing.

Her father had that quality of desert and mountain men that he could sleep when he wished, and he slept now, curled up on the sand.

Several times she got up from where she sat and looked around, careful to show no movement to any possible watcher below. Already she had acquired from her father those habits of care and eternal watchfulness so essential to the wilderness life among hostile Indians.

The sky grew pale, then the red arrows of the sun opened the heavens to the gold that followed. The shadows fled, somewhere a bird sang, the song crystal clear in the morning air. The sky became blue, the cacti turned from gray to green, and the morning was with them.

Her father still slept; and now, relaxed in the shade of a boulder, his face for the first time looked old, and for the first time she thought what this must mean to him, to be starting over again at his age, to be making a new life...and for her.

There was strength in him still, a resilient strength as of some kind of strange steel that resists all corrosion, so that he lived on, seemingly timeless, everlasting. Yet he was not...and she knew some of his haste, knew the reason for it.

The sky was fully light now, and when she looked around again she saw an Indian sitting on a horse. He was not over a hundred yards away, and he was looking straight toward them.

Considine was riding with the Kiowa. The Apaches, who were stalking the two ahead of them, had not held to the trail, but they were moving westward. Considine remembered vaguely some story about a Yuma Indian who had taken an Apache girl to wife and had become a noted warrior among them. If that was the case, it might account for the Apaches ranging so far west.

The four riders had been following the trail only a short time when they found the broken shoe. From there on, the tracks were of two people who walked, leading the horse. Only occasionally did they ride, obviously saving the horse as much as possib.e for whatever might lie ahead.

Considine closed off his thoughts from Spanyer and Lennie. They would make it...somehow.

Tonight he and the boys would hole up in that cave on Castle Dome.

West of the Dome there was a saddle by which they could cross into the valley beyond, and then follow Silver Creek to the east side of the mountains. There were a couple of springs down there. It might be better to stay west and avoid those springs...but there was good water there.

He could tell that the horse Spanyer led was limping badly, and would be no use at all if they did have to run for it. He swore to himself...nobody looked at him, or said anything. The story of the tracks could be read by them all.

Hardy mopped his face and tried to ease his position in the saddle. Their eyes were constantly moving, searching, watching. They were carrying more money than they had ever had in their lives, or were likely to have again.

"Man," Hardy said suddenly, "I'd like to have seen their faces back in Obaro!"

Nobody replied...somehow robbing the bank in Obaro seemed a small thing today.

Hardy stared at the others belligerently, but they ignored him. Well, nobody else had ever done it, had they? And *they* had. He could tell the girls down in Sonora that he was one of those who stood up the bank in Obaro. That would make them sit up and listen!

Only he was not convincing himself. Somehow, the robbery of the bank had dwindled in importance.

Their eyes were reading the trail sign: an old man and a young girl were leading a crippled horse through Indian country.

"The posse might help them," Dutch said, voicing a thought that was in all their minds.

"Take 'em off our trail," Hardy said, with false cheer-fulness.

The four rode on in silence, dusty, tired, and wary. Behind them was a posse, before them a war party of In-dians, south of them the inviting border where there was a ranch they knew of, where they could hole up for a few days before going back toward Sonoita and then down to Hermosillo.

Suddenly a flock of quail burst from the brush some fifty yards ahead and to the left.

Dust lifted from an empty trail. The four riders were gone...vanished. The explosion of those quail had been warning enough, and they had acted with the split-second speed they had acquired by years of danger.

From the lip of a dry wash, Considine held his Win-chester steady while his eyes searched for an enemy. Dutch had gone into the same wash some fifty yards up. The others were nowhere in sight.

For a short space of time nothing happened. Considine glanced around at his horse, surveyed the wash behind him, and waited. His skin itched from the dust and sweat, his tongue touched his dry lips. He squinted his eyes into the hot bright day and searched for an Indian. And then a rifle's flat statement ended the silence.

The shot came from their side, and it brought a dozen quick replies.

Hardy came walking placidly down the wash behind Considine and grinned up at him. "That Kiowa, he sees better than any man I know. I'll lay you five to one he notched one."

He unlimbered his rifle and crawled up beside Con-sidine.

"The Kiowa's not a dozen feet from where he was when those quail went up. He's got him a nest among the rocks."

There was no sign of Dutch. The Kiowa fired again, but nobody replied to his shot.

Considine mopped his forehead to keep the sweat out of his eyes. The earth felt hot, and the temperature here against the sand was much hotter than it was when one was riding. His shirt was soaked with sweat.

The Kiowa shot again, and an Indian reared up suddenly and threw his rifle out in front of him; then he toppled forward over a creosote bush.

Silence followed, a silence in which there was only sand and sun, and the smell of their own stale clothing.

Suddenly there was a chorus of shrill yells and half a dozen Indians came from the sand and rushed the Kiowa's hide-out. All three men fired from the wash, and two Indians fell. Considine triggered his rifle swiftly again, and in the moment following his shot, Dutch fired from up the wash.

The Kiowa had deliberately baited the Apaches into an attack to open them up for the guns of his friends. The Indians probably thought they had fled.

Minutes passed, long, slow minutes, and nothing happened. Then the Kiowa came into sight, riding his horse. He drew up, looking around, and the three men came over the edge of the wash, leading their horses. Dutch was bleeding from a scratch on his face.

"Shale," he said; "ricocheted from a bullet."

It was their only injury. They found no Indians, not even dead ones, but there was blood.

"Two," the Kiowa said, "maybe three."

The Apache was a good fighting man, but no fool. Against the kind of shooting they had faced, this was not the time nor the place. But these Apaches were not the same bunch that followed Spanyer and Lennie. Perhaps thirty or more had broken up into small parties because of the water.

89

"They were coming here," the Kiowa said. "There is water there." He indicated a dry waterfall and, turning his horse, he rode to it and swung down. Dropping to his knees, he dug into the sand. Soon the sand was wet, and then there was water. They drank, then one by one they allowed their horses to drink as the water seeped into the hole.

"There is often water in such places, but after a rain it is sure," the Kiowa said.

A few clouds drifted across the sky, making islands of shadow upon the desert. There was no smoke.

"An old hide-out's up yonder," Dutch said suddenly, "up on High Lonesome."

"Pete Runyon knows it."

"Do you think he's still coming?" Hardy asked.

"You can just bet he is." Considine glanced at their back trail. "I can say for sure that he's a persistent kind of man."

"Does he know about the cave on Castle Dome?"

"I doubt it...but he might."

Dutch rolled a smoke, letting his huge body relax slowly. "Only the old ones know it," he said. "I told Considine." He touched his tongue to the cigarette paper. "Spanyer probably knows it, and he knows about High Lonesome."

"We turn south right up ahead," the Kiowa said. "Beyond that peak."

They squinted against the sun. Before them were the tracks of the man and the girl and, almost wiping them out, the tracks of the Indians.

Dutch stared at the tracks, then blinked his eyes against the smart of the salt from the sweat trickling into his eyes.

Considine looked up toward High Lonesome.

TEN

Before Lennie could wake her father, the Indian on the horse had vanished.

"Don't worry," he said to her. "You saw it all right."

Under the hot morning sky the desert mountains looked like a crumpled sheet of dusty copper, dotted here and there with clumps of green brush.

Dave Spanyer had studied their situation in the vague light before he closed his eyes, and he knew they could be approached from all sides. But on two sides there was almost no cover, and therefore he expected the attack from there.

Any sensible defender would be watching the approaches that allowed for cover, and Spanyer was sure the Indians would show themselves there. But the real attack would come from the quarter least expected.

A master of concealment, the Apache knew the art of

91

guerrilla fighting as no people before or since. Moreover, he lived in a country that provided little in the way of natural cover, and he had learned the art of winning battles in such a country.

The old man placed Lennie where she could do the best job of covering any attack from the obvious sides, and took the other sides himself. Fortunately, their circle of rocks was small, and the hollow was sufficient to allow cover for the horse.

"That Considine..." Spanyer began, and after a pause he continued, "He might make you a good man."

Tears came to her eyes, and in that moment Dave Spanyer was closer to his daughter than ever before. She no longer had even hope of seeing Considine again, but the brief moment with him had been her only moment of love, and she did love him.

Suddenly, with that one sentence, Dave Spanyer had broken down whatever barrier there was between his daughter and himself. In her own mind she could see them together, these two men whom she loved, and herself.

Looking out over the rocks and the mountain around them, she thought of the tired, stoop-shouldered man who was her father. He was oddly puritanical, not alone in his care for her, but in his viewpoint toward women in general. A man who had known nothing but loneliness since her mother died. Somehow, some way, she must make that up to him.

There was no movement out among the clumps of brush. Lennie held her rifle ready. She had killed game, but only when it was necessary for food; she had never shot at a man. It gave her a terribly frightened feeling to think of it...and to think that within a few minutes she might be dead herself.

Her eyes searched the terrain, shifting from one rock or clump to another, moving slowly across the area before her. She was aware that movement is first detected, and best detected, from the corners of the eyes.

She saw nothing, no movement.... And then there was, a faint stirring on the ground, and she saw it was a brown foot that drew in behind a bush.

She judged the distance carefully, considered the bush. There was no place he could get to quickly from where he had been, so she sighted into the bush a little to the right of where she had seen the foot. She took a deep breath, let out a little of it, then steadied the rifle on the target. The muzzle wavered, and she steadied it again, and all the time she was taking up slack on the trigger. Suddenly the rifle leaped in her hands.

The foot stiffened out, then slowly drew back part way, and remained there.

"That's one, Pa."

"Good girl."

Three Indians rose at once and started toward her. She fired...too quick. All three disappeared into the brush, a good fifty feet closer.

Spanyer had not turned his head, and suddenly they came out of the desert where nothing had been a minute before. He fired carefully...*once...twice...a third time.*

One down, and one possible.

He wiped the sweat from his eyes. There was nothing in sight, nothing anywhere. They were out there, but they were invisible.

He wanted a drink desperately, for his mouth was suddenly very dry, but he dared not move from his post. They would get close, for there was no possible way to keep them off for long.

He glanced at the sun. It was still early. How long had they been watching out there? He shot suddenly at a suspicion of movement, then threw a wild shot into a vacant area to let them know that he knew what they were doing.

It came to him suddenly that he would never see the sun go down this day.

Well, he had lived a full life, if a hard one. What worried him was Lennie. She deserved better than this, to die in a lonely circle of rocks, die by a bullet...for he would save a bullet for her. He owed her that, more than anything. He had given her life; now, to save her from what might come, he would also give her death.

His eyes were red-rimmed from staring. Lennie...God knew he had wanted better than this for her. What kind of a man was he that he had got her into such a position? He had expected to die this way himself...all the odds were in favor of it—either in some such place as this, or in the dust of a western street, or on the sawdust of a barroom floor.

But Lennie was young, her life only just begun. Only the other day, only hours ago, she had first looked at a man with anything but casual interest, and he, her father, had almost destroyed even her dream of him. And Dave Spanyer, frontiersman and outlaw, knew what it was to dream. He had done some dreaming himself.

Why did the young think that dreams were only for them? The old dream also, with less hope, less anticipation, yet they dream.

And he had dreamed for Lennie. He had dreamed of a good marriage for her, a good home.

He dried his palms by running his hands down the front of his pants. "You all right, Lennie?" he asked.

"All right, Pa."

"If we can stand them off until night, we might slip out of here and get away."

They might...but the chances were not good. And the chances of surviving that long were not good either. He knew how slight those chances were. Those Indians were not going to take much more time, and they had cost them blood. Those Indians had patience, but they also

HIGH LONESOME

would be eager, each one of them, to be the one to capture the girl.

"Make every shot count," he said, and then to give her something to die with, he added, "I shouldn't have been so rough. I think Considine is a good man. I hope he comes west."

"Thanks, Pa." She ran her eyes over the rocks and brush. "He was good to me...he really was. I...I think he liked me."

"He'd just better!" Then Spanyer was silent. Well, why not? If he was to have a son-in-law, why not Considine? He would understand Considine...they would understand each other. "Of course he liked you! I could see it."

Nothing moved...but they were out there. Dave Spanyer thought of his wife....Was she watching them now? Did the dead know how the living fared? He had never thought much about such things before.

God, but the sun was hot! It was high now, blazing down upon them, and there was no shelter.

"Californy's quite a place, Lennie. We'll get ourselves a place there. I've been thinking...maybe I could get word through to Mexico...invite that young man to come callin'."

There was silence.

"You all right, Lennie?"

"Yes, Pa, but—"

The report of her rifle took over. She shot rapidly, three times, and then he saw an Indian come out of the grass where there did not seem to be cover for a rattler, and he shot him through the chest before he was off the ground. He could smell powder smoke, and fear...yes, he could smell the fear that was in him.

"Get one?" he asked.

"No."

"They lost one over here."

95

He snaked the canteen to him and took a quick drink, sloshing the water around inside his mouth before he swallowed. He fought off the desire to drink and drink and drink, and put the canteen down.

Tension and fear always made a man thirsty. After a fight sometimes he would drink until it seemed there was no bottom in him.

He glanced at the sun. They would be lucky if they lasted until noon.

He looked around at Lennie. She was all right, but their horse was down. A bullet had got him, and he was kicking out his last breath.

Well, he would have been hard to get out of here at night, anyway.

But Spanyer felt something go out of him. How could they tackle the desert on foot? And it was a nasty piece of travel before they could get to Yuma.

He lifted his rifle, searching the brush out there, and waiting. How much longer now? An hour? Two hours?

"It isn't far now," Dutch said. "We can make the cave by sundown."

They started on again, and then they heard the far-off solid blast of a shot.

They drew up sharply, tense and listening. Then more shots, a lull, and another shot.

Dutch spat into the dust, avoiding the others' eyes. "They're up on High Lonesome. I know that place."

Another shot, and then a ragged volley. That last would be the Indians.

They sat their mounts, staring at the hills. Hardy looked away toward the border. It was close now. If the pursuit was still after them, it would end when they turned south, for there was small chance of any pursuit catching up before they were safely across.

Sixty thousand dollars...in gold!

Considine looked at the mountains. He felt all hollow and empty inside. The damned old cantankerous fool! What got into a man that he would get his daughter into something like this?

But he knew. Spanyer was running away. He wanted to take her somewhere where he would not be known for what he was, he wanted to give her a chance, a start in life.

No start in life now. If they were cornered up there, off the usual trails, there was no hope of rescue. There was no hope of anything.

The posse would be closing in by now. They had probably brought extra horses. Trust Runyon to think of that. And they might have been riding most of the night. By the time the posse got here, Spanyer and Lennie would be gone.

"It ain't far to the border now," Hardy said. "I can almost see that Mex gal's eyes a-shining!"

That old hide-out on High Lonesome…it was a good place to defend—if they had made it that far. But it was a good place for four or five to defend, not two.

Three…even three might have a chance.

Considine remembered the firm wet body he had held in his arms, the quiet, proud eyes, the eyes that had waited while he held her, confident of him.

Damn it, what did she have to be confident about? What did she expect of a man, anyway? And how could she be so sure of *him?*

He fumbled with the piggin strings that tied the bag on his saddle. He tossed the sack to Dutch. "We'll split this south of the border!" He swung his horse around. "You'd better high-tail it, boys! I'm a damned fool!"

He wheeled the big black and went up High Lonesome on a dead run.

Dust rose and settled; it drifted back from where he had gone, and settled slowly in the hot, heavy air. They sat their saddles, listening to the drum of hoofs fading away.

"Why, that damned, hare-brained fool!" Dutch said. "He'll go blasting right into the middle of them! That's no way to fight 'Paches!"

The Kiowa wiped off the mechanism of his rifle and said nothing to anyone, but the Kiowa never had anything to say. He was a square, solid young man, with a square, solid face and black eyes that were flat and steady.

Dutch gathered his reins. "All right, south to the border then."

The Kiowa looked at him, then slid his rifle back in the scabbard.

"If he rides into the middle of 'em," Hardy said, "God help the Apaches!"

Dutch had let his horse walk four steps. Now he turned and tossed to Hardy the bag Considine had given him, then the one he himself had carried. Then he jumped his horse, not at the canyon opening but at another draw that led up into the hills. It was a worse climb, but it would put him up there almost as fast as Considine could make it.

Considine ran his horse for half a mile, then slowed to a trot. You could kill a horse running it in the heat like this, and he had a feeling he was going to need a good horse if he got out of here alive.

There was small chance of an ambush in the canyon unless they heard him coming, and they would not be expecting an attack. He carried his Winchester in his right hand, and he rode carefully.

Ahead of him he heard the flat, hard report of a rifle, then several shots close together. Suddenly he went fast up that last hard climb and was racing his horse across the grassy meadow toward the hide-out.

Another shot sounded, and he wheeled his horse, standing in the stirrups. They had stopped short of the hideout, then. They were there...in that circle of rocks!

An Indian came out of the rocks near him and threw a rifle to his shoulder, but before Considine could get his own rifle up, a shot nailed the Indian and he fell over the rocks into the grass.

Startled, Considine looked around to see Dutch sliding his horse down a steep gravel bank. "Run for it!" Dutch yelled. "I'll cover for you!"

Considine slammed the Winchester back in the scabbard and grabbed his six-shooter. He put spurs to the big black and went across the flat in a wild run, reins hanging loose. Behind him, Dutch was laying down a heavy fire from his Winchester.

He saw an Indian dead ahead of him lift a rifle to fire, and then the big black was riding him down, the terrible hoofs tearing the Indian's body as they trampled him under foot. Considine fired and fired again. He saw another Indian fall, and then he felt the black's muscles bunch under him and knew he was going down.

Kicking free of the stirrups, he grabbed the saddlebags with their spare ammunition and as the horse fell he left him, hit the ground, and rolled over. He saw an Indian break cover near him and start for him, and then a bullet from the rock circle ahead stopped him in mid-stride.

Considine knew they would have marked where he fell, so he lay still, flattened out in the grass. Behind him he heard Dutch firing.

Suddenly the shooting stopped, and the echoes cannonaded off down the canyon and lost themselves in the still, hot afternoon.

He smelled the sun-hot grass under his nostrils, smelled the crushed creosote brush near him, the warm, good smell of the earth under him, and he knew he loved life as never before.

He lay very still. Dutch was no longer shooting. Had they gotten the big fellow? He doubted it.... Dutch would die hard...and long.

A bee, undisturbed by the fighting, buzzed near a cactus blossom. Considine rolled on his side and emptied the shells from his pistol and reloaded. Then he thrust a couple of shells into the magazine of the Winchester. The '73 would carry seventeen bullets, and he would need them.

He dearly wanted to lift his head and locate himself, get his exact position, but he dared not. In this deadly game the first to move was often the first to die, and he did not want to die. He did not want to die at all.

The Kiowa had sat very still, waiting. He glanced out of the corners of his eyes at Hardy. "You rode partners with Considine," he said.

"That's why I'm going to look after his share. He will want it if he ever gets out of there alive."

"Always said you had no guts."

Hardy glared at the breed. The Kiowa was taunting him, but there was no malice in the taunt. He just seemed to be waiting for something he knew would happen.

Hardy felt cold and empty inside. He knew what fighting Apaches meant, and he had seen what they did to men they captured alive. He had fought them before this, had seen his friends die in their hands.

It gave him a sick feeling to think of it...he knew he was afraid of them.

Considine was a fool, but then there was something between Considine and that girl. He had seen the way they looked at each other.

He took the saddlebags and tossed them to the Kiowa. "Cut it four ways and wait for us!" He wheeled his horse sharply and lit out on the trail Dutch had taken.

The Kiowa chuckled. None of his three companions had ever heard him chuckle.

He tied the bags in place, then turned his horse into the mountains. He took his time, thinking it out. He was more Indian than white now, and he knew what he was doing.

But he laughed when he reached the crest.

He had no God, no people that were really his own; he had no wife, no hero, no brother anywhere. He was a man who rode alone, even when in company with others. But he liked to fight and he liked men who fought, and he knew that if Hardy had not gone he would have killed him.

When he reached a place where he could look into the basin of High Lonesome there was nothing to see, nothing to hear. The afternoon was breathless. The grass stood motionless under the sun—and then within the circle of rocks he saw sunlight on a rifle barrel.

He watched, and presently he saw the girl. She was alive, then. And the man, too.

He could see no sign of Considine, of Dutch, nor of Hardy.

He loosened the reins and rode down the mountain, a square, dark man the color of the desert near lava, sitting easy in the saddle. Horse and man seemed one.

His Winchester was held out from his body. The flat black eyes were alert. He felt the sweat on his neck and chest.

Suddenly he chuckled again. He would have liked to paint his face. After all, he was an Indian and he was riding into a fight.

His sombrero was tilted back a little, and he swung his horse over to an easier descent, and then he saw two Indians crouched close together among some brush.

He drew up, not looking directly at them for fear his continued gaze would attract their attention. He lifted the rifle and sighted down the barrel, one eye closed, the other eye centering the muzzle on an Indian's spine.

He sighted first at one Indian, then at the other. A fly buzzed near him and he brushed it away. His horse shifted its weight under him and he held still, waiting. When its feet were planted solid again he settled the stock against his shoulder, took a quick sight, eased back on the trigger...the rifle leaped like a thing alive, and the Indian

101

screamed...a shrill, horrible scream. The second one leaped up, but the sight was already on him and a tearing bullet opened his throat and laid it red to the sky.

Lowering his rifle, the Kiowa walked his horse on down the hill.

ELEVEN

Considine hugged the earth, but he drew one knee up slowly and dug his toe into the sand. His right hand slid the rifle forward. He tried to estimate the distance to a heap of brush and rocks just a bit nearer to the hide-out.

He heard a rifle boom behind him…that would be Dutch's heavier rifle. From somewhere farther away, he heard another shot, then another. Suddenly he felt a strange warmth within him…that would be Hardy, or the Kiowa.

Digging the toe a little deeper, he pushed up suddenly and went forward in a charging run. He made four fast steps, then hit the ground and rolled over four times. He brought up behind the rocks with the memory of bullets snapping about his ears.

Considine lay still, gathering his strength and wind. Above and to his left, a little farther in front of him, he heard another shot. The rocks behind which he was hidden concealed all movement.

Sweat and dust streaked his face. His skin prickled and itched. The sun was hot on his back. He slid his rifle forward and searched for a target. Now, through the rocks, he could see the place where Lennie and her father were...only the smallest crack offered a view.

One more quick dash...a bullet from behind smashed against a rock ahead of him and he slid back hurriedly, his face stinging from granite fragments.

He waited, and for a long time there was no sound. This was the hardest part of battle, the waiting, the uncertainty of what might have happened or might be happening elsewhere.

Were they all dead? Was Lennie dead? Was Spanyer dead? And what of Dutch?

He glanced at his own brown hand, gripping the rifle. It was a strong hand, skilled with rope and branding iron, a hand that had used an axe, a saw, many kinds of tools. It was a hand that could build as well as destroy, and with a kind of odd surprise he realized he had been and was a destroyer. He had been destructive of the labor of other men, and what had begun in the excitement of youth, almost as a lark had turned into an evil thing.

And he had nothing—not a cabin of his own, not an acre of ground, not even a horse. For the big black was dead behind him.

There was a sudden burst of firing and he left the ground as if shot from a gun himself, knowing instinctively that any Indian who was watching where he lay would be disconcerted, diverted by the sound.

He rushed, and saw an Indian rise up before him. He smashed upward with the barrel of the Winchester and took the Indian in the throat, the sight ripping a gash even as the muzzle jammed up into the juncture of throat and jaw.

Whipping the rifle down and round, he swung the butt with a solid *chunk* against the Indian's skull, a short, wicked stroke.

The Apache, a squat man with an evil face, crumpled before him, and Considine sprang past him. He dropped a hand to the top of a rock and vaulted over and came down within the circle, and as he landed he saw Dave Spanyer facing him, his rifle trained on his stomach.

And Spanyer had said that the next time he saw Considine he would kill him.

For an instant they stared at each other, and then Dave Spanyer lowered his rifle. If anything happened to him, this man would have his daughter, and suddenly deep within him he knew this was good...this man would do.

"Pull up a chair, son. I'm afraid there's enough for all."

Considine grinned. "I'll do that, Dave. But we've company coming...unless they ran into too many Indians."

Dutch was next. He came charging his horse, vaulting the rocks at the lowest place, and throwing himself to the ground. There was an angry red gash alongside of his neck, and his sleeve was torn and bloody.

Spanyer looked at him affectionately. "You never could stay out of a fracas...and nobody was ever more welcome."

Dutch moved to the rocks and carried an extra bandolier of cartridges with him. He found a place and settled down for a fight. And then out of a canyon mouth came Hardy.

They knew the horse, even though they could not see the man. The horse was running all out, nostrils spread wide, and Hardy was clinging to the flank, Indian fashion, with one hand and a foot.

Even as the horse seemed about to sweep past the hide-out, Hardy let go and came sailing into the open space, one boot flying off by itself. He skidded to a halt, then looked down at a big hole in his sock.

He grinned widely at Lennie. "Got to speak to my women folks about that!"

He turned and limped to the barrier. From that barrier four men now faced outward, awaiting the attack. And none came.

The basin on High Lonesome was a lovely place, and for outlaws it had long been an almost perfect hide-away. There was water, there was grass, and without doubt there was game. In some more peaceful time some wandering man would stop and build a home here, and start a ranch. He would stay, rear children, sink roots deep within the sparse soil.

In this place something would belong, something not hidden, not stolen, something built by work and strength. And that man would sit quietly of an evening with his chores done and see his own cattle grazing out there where Indians now lay.

That would be after the Apaches were gone, or when they had found peace themselves. It would be when men no longer rode by the gun and lived by the gun.

"Smoke," Spanyer said suddenly.

Their eyes followed his pointing finger, to where a tall column of smoke lifted easily into the sky, a smoke that broke, then broke again. A signal calling more Indians, calling them in for the kill.

Behind them a stick broke, and as one man they turned.

Lennie was building a fire. "I thought you'd want some coffee," she said, "and there's a little meat."

Considine glanced at her, and then away, his throat tight. She was so much the daughter of Dave Spanyer, and too much the child of rolling wagons and Indian fighting not to know what awaited them; yet she went quietly about the business of making coffee, a woman's business. But her rifle lay close at hand.

What man would not want such a woman? Not one to follow only, but to stand beside him during the dark days, to work with him, plan with him, share with him, making their life a whole thing together.

High on the mountainside still, the Kiowa lay in the brush, his horse concealed. He had crawled after leaving his horse, but he carried his saddlebags, his canteen, and his rifle.

He had found a place where there were no rocks and but little grass. The earth was discolored by a scattering of rusty, quartz-streaked rock. It was perfect cover for him, and he settled himself deeper.

From where he lay he could see the hide-out, but he could see nothing within it. Occasionally he saw an Indian.

It was growing late. Already the afternoon sun was over the western hills. That sun was still hot and bright, the air was very clear. But night would come, and the Kiowa could wait.

Waiting was the first thing an Indian learned, and now, more than ever, the Kiowa was an Indian. He carried his white blood casually, without ever thinking of it. He was a man of simple, elemental tastes, taking food, whiskey, and women as he found them, and when he did not have them he neither fretted nor worried. He knew there was an end to everything. So one waited.

Lying here like this in the sparse grass he liked best of all. The sun was warm, the position good, and soon he would be fighting...if he decided to fight.

Yet that decision had never been his—it was made long ago, it was deep in his flesh, in his blood, bred deeply into the bone. It was the manner of man he was.

And being a true fighting man he knew there was a time to fight and a time not to fight.

He could have killed several Indians during the time he lay where he now was, but the time was not yet. He could wait, and when the proper time came he would do what was necessary.

From his pocket he took a dusty bit of jerked beef and, biting off a piece, he began to chew. He rolled it in his wide jaws, letting it soak with saliva, and chewed it with his strong white teeth. From where he lay he was visible to nothing but the buzzards, but they were not interested in him...yet.

The Kiowa watched the shadows crawl out from the cracks and the canyons, and watched the sunlight retreat up the mountainside and crown the ridges with golden spires and balustrades.

Coolness came to the desert. He watched the signal smoke rise to call more Indians, but he merely chewed his beef and waited.

Fainter smoke came from the hide-out. The girl was alive, then. No man would take time to cook in such a place at such a time. This was a woman's work, a woman who even under stress did not forget her men or the work there was to do. She was not spoiled, this one. She was a man's woman.

The Kiowa did not know the word for love. His people had songs, but they were songs of war, and he had no books or poetry to condition his mind for love. He knew what a woman was worth by the looks of her body and the way she worked. And sometimes there was another feeling, the warm, pleasant feeling when a certain girl was near.

He had known that feeling several times, once for a girl in Mexico, and a long time later for a Navajo girl in whose hogan he had stayed for a time. When he rode away he felt strangely lost and alone without her and he had returned, but in the meantime she had been killed by a grizzly she accidentally cornered in a canyon.

He had gone to the place where she had been killed and stood there for a while and smoked a cigarette, and then he got on his horse and rode away and never went back to that part of the country again.

He had started rustling cattle because he was hungry. He killed a beef he found loose on the plains when he was nearly starved. Two cowhands found him and drew their guns on him. The trouble was they drew too slow and one of them was falling from his saddle before the gun cleared leather, and the other made it back to the home ranch with a bullet through his chest.

They had come after him then, a whole posse of them, and he circled around and reached their ranch while they were gone and he butchered a beef in their dooryard and broiled a steak on their own fire. Then he took what supplies he needed—a new Winchester rifle and a hundred rounds of ammunition, as well as a couple of Navajo blankets.

Ten years later he met Considine, and he stayed with him because Considine was faster with a gun than he was, was as good a tracker, and as good a horseman. Also, Considine was quiet, confident, and careful, and the Kiowa understood those qualities.

Now he watched the basin turn from twilight into darkness. It was a beautiful place, if one forgot the Indians, but being an Indian, he did not forget.

As he waited for darkness he located one by one the hiding places of the Indians. Most of them would bunch together now, but a few would remain where they were, and that pleased him.

He watched the first stars appear, and then he got up.

"I'm glad you're here," she said.

"Well..."—he was at a loss for words—"I came."

They were standing close together in the darkness, each conscious of the other, yet wanting no more than this now.

The call of an owl quavered lonesomely in the night. Then again.

"Don't the Indians frighten them away?" Lennie asked.

"That was an Indian."

"That owl? How can you tell?"

"Something in the tone. Any sound a man makes will echo. A real owl's call has some quality a man can't put into it...its call doesn't echo."

Suddenly there was a shrill, high-pitched scream, breaking off sharply. Lennie turned in startled horror.

"What...what was *that?*"

"A man died."

Her father came up beside them in the darkness. "Did you hear that?" he asked.

"Uh-huh."

There was no further sound. After a few minutes Considine said to Spanyer, just loud enough for Hardy to hear too. "The Kiowa is out there."

"The Injun?" Dave Spanyer looked around. "Could be." His eyes searched for Considine's in the darkness. "You think they got him?"

"No, he got one of them...maybe more. Maybe only one of them had a chance to yell."

There was no further sound. The wind rose, and after a while Hardy came down from his perch and wakened Dutch. Dave Spanyer took Considine's place, and the two younger men turned in.

Lennie watched them roll up in their blankets, then prepared stew for the two older men.

Considine opened his eyes in the gray of morning. The sky was overcast and dull. He sat up, combing his dark hair with his fingers, then reaching for his boots. Spanyer was standing guard at a place where he could watch a wide area, and Lennie was asleep on her blankets. Dutch was nowhere in sight.

The grass seemed gray, the trees were a wall of darkness, the brush was black. It was shivering cold.

Standing up, Considine slung his gun belt about his lean hips and picked up his Winchester. He checked his guns, one by one.

"Quiet?"

Spanyer nodded. "Yeah...too quiet."

Considine saw Dutch then. The big man was wedged between two rocks, somewhat forward of their position. Dutch motioned and Considine ducked behind a rock and went up to him, crouching low.

"What do you make of that?"

Dutch indicated an Indian, standing bolt upright and still on the edge of the brush. He seemed, at this distance, unnaturally tall.

The Indian made no move. Considine stared hard, straining his eyes to see better. "Dutch," he whispered, "that Indian's dead."

"Dead?"

"Look...he's tied to a tree, his feet off the ground."

"Is it the Kiowa?"

"Not heavy enough in the chest. No, it's one of them." Considine glanced at Dutch. "I figure the Kiowa's had a busy night."

They watched in silence. A gust of wind brushed the grass and bent it. A tumbleweed detached itself from the brush and rolled over several times, then stopped in the clearing near the dead Indian. Another gust, and it rolled over again, then again.

113

Both men studied the dead Indian.... The wind blew, and the tumbleweed rolled over again.

Considine shifted his eyes from the dead Indian to the tumbleweed. It was a great, dark clump of weed, large, but no larger than some others he had seen. As he watched, it rolled over again.

"That's big enough," he said aloud, "to hide a man."

Dutch lifted his rifle, but Considine touched his arm. "Hold everything," he said. "I've got an idea."

Dutch waited, watching.

The wind struck again and the tumbleweed rolled over, bringing it within twenty yards of the rocks where they crouched. A gust caught it and rolled it once more.

"I think," Considine said, "we're going to have company."

Suddenly a gun flashed at the edge of the brush. Both Considine and Dutch fired at the flash, and in that instant the Kiowa broke from the tumbleweed, and lunged for the rocks.

"Maybe thirty out there," the Kiowa said. "I kill two."

Spanyer fired suddenly, the sound of his rifle cut sharply across by the report of a second.

"You boys come to breakfast," Spanyer said. "We're havin' company."

The Apaches came with a rush, and Considine held his rifle centered on the chest of a big Indian who looked more like a Yuma than an Apache. He held it, then fired.

The Indian was caught in mid-stride. One foot pawed at the air, then he turned on the ball of the other foot as though doing some grotesque ballet, and he fell and lay still.

The attack broke, but the attackers did not run; they dropped to concealment on the ground.

The sound of firing ceased, and the air was still. The gray clouds hung low, hiding the morning. The dark red peaks of the mountains were touched by a shroud of mist or cloud. The grass bent before the wind.

Dutch fired suddenly, and they heard the ugly *thud* of a bullet striking flesh.

Considine built himself a cigarette and shoved a cartridge into the magazine of his rifle. This time the Indians would rush from a closer position. He thought he heard a faint, almost inaudible scratching sound. Listening, he heard nothing more. Some small animal?

When they came again it was suddenly, and from all sides. Considine whipped his rifle to his shoulder and felt the slam of the recoil and the bellow in his ears. The smell of gunpowder drifted into his nostrils. He leveled his rifle desperately, firing again and again.

All around there was heavy firing. A bullet whacked sharply against the boulder at his side and ricocheted with an angry, frustrated whine. The attack broke and the sound rolled away along the cliffs under the low clouds.

Considine turned at a coughing sound. Hardy was down, choking on his own blood. Lennie was beside him.

"You...you stick to Considine...he's the...best. Hope you make it."

Considine came over to him. "You're a good man, Hardy. I'm glad we've had this time together."

"This'll save somebody...better a bullet than a rope."

A few spatters of rain fell. Considine went back to the rocks. The firing continued, only intermittent shooting now, but the Indians had the range, and they had found positions where they could fire into the circle of rocks, so every bullet was a danger. The openings had been located and they were firing into them.

Considine shifted his feet. He smelled of sweat and his unwashed clothing, and he needed a shave. He was a man who had never liked a stubble of beard.

He felt a tug at his shirt, and saw the shoulder was

split and a trace of blood where the bullet had burned. He caught a stir in the brush and fired, and instantly three bullets smashed against the rock, one of them glancing upward with a wicked, snarling whine.

Lennie brought him coffee again. "This is the last of it," she said. "And there's only half a canteen of water."

In the east the clouds had broken a little and there was sunlight on the far-off peaks. "How's Hardy?" he asked.

"He's gone."

Her voice sounded very thin, and he glanced at her quickly. She looked drawn and pale, and her eyes were unnaturally large. He dropped a hand to her shoulder and squeezed it gently.

He gulped his coffee and handed her the cup; she looked quickly up into his eyes, then turned away.

An hour of desultory firing passed. Nobody on their side was hurt, but every shot was a near miss. They themselves did not kill anyone, or even see a good target.

Suddenly, from away back, they came on horseback. They charged from the brush on a dead run, with only a moment's warning from the pounding hoofs, and as the defenders opened fire the Indians close by rose up suddenly and threw themselves over the stones of the circle.

Considine fired, and saw a horse spill headlong, throwing his rider; then a bloody Indian came over the rocks. Considine, gripping his rifle by the barrel and the action, ruined his face with a wicked butt stroke. He swung it back, fired at another, and was knocked sprawling by an Indian who came through a gap in the rocks. He lost his grip on his rifle, drew a .44, and shot the Indian as he crouched over him, tomahawk in hand.

A bullet caught Dutch and the big man fell back against the rocks, gripping an Indian's throat in his huge hands. The warrior struggled wildly, desperately, but Dutch clung to his throat with crushing force.

Dutch went to his knees, still gripping the dead Indian's throat, and the attack was over again—only Dutch was down on his knees, his shirt drenched in blood, his big face gone an ugly gray. He started to speak, but could not make it. He died like that, on his knees with the Indian's throat in his hands.

Two gone...and the day was young.

THIRTEEN

Under a low gray sky and a spattering of rain the posse, now mounted on fresh horses, pushed along the trail. The outlaws were undoubtedly far ahead, and might have reached the border, but there was no slacking off in the pursuit. The honor of Obaro was at stake, and Pete Runyon himself had been flaunted.

"Wherever they are," Ollie Weedin said, "they're in trouble. I just can't figure Apaches this far west."

"Renegades...mixed tribes."

Pete Runyon was worried. There were too many Indians out, and his band numbered only twenty-five—a strong force under ordinary circumstances, but the situation was far from ordinary. It was one thing to lead a posse after outlaws, but quite another if he got his friends killed by marauding Apaches.

He turned the idea over in his mind and reluctantly

118

decided that if there were no results by noon they would return home. And it was not far from noon now.

He said as much to Weedin.

"Maybe that's the best thing," Weedin agreed. "But a man hates to give up."

Pete Runyon studied the situation and tried to recall everything he knew about Considine. The others were also known men, but it would be Considine he would have to outguess if the outlaws were to be caught and the money recovered.

Without doubt Considine knew the country as far as the border, and from all reports Dutch did also. And Considine had daring enough to ride right off into the heart of Indian country. Where four men might slip through if they knew the *tinajas* and the seeps, a large party like the posse could not.

Weedin considered the matter and agreed with Runyon. "If he turns toward the border we might as well give up. What I can't understand is why he is so far west if it's the border that he figures on."

Mack Arrow, the Indian tracker who was riding ahead checking the trail, turned his horse and waited for the others to come up.

"No turn," he said. "Follow man and girl."

Runyon scowled thoughtfully and studied the tracks indicated by the Indian. They had noticed the tracks of the couple some time back, and they had seen a few of their tracks around the Chavez store, where they were sure Considine had kept his spare horses.

The safety of Considine lay south across the border, so why were they continuing on west? Runyon thought this over, remembering Considine. He looked over at Arrow.

"Are you sure that's a girl?" he asked.

"Small tracks, light foot, quick step. It is a girl, all right. I see where she sleep, also. Very small, like girl or child."

119

If Mack Arrow said it was a girl, it was a girl. The Indian added, "First man and girl, then many Indians, then Considine and other men."

Weedin eased himself in the saddle and bit off a corner of his plug of tobacco. "We know Considine," he said quietly; "what else would you expect? He must have seen those folks back there at Honey's place...then he sees the Indians are on their trail."

"Two people on one horse," Pete Runyon said. "Believe me, they'd have no chance."

Mack Arrow indicated the ground. "Men talk, horses very active...want to go. Then one man goes off...the others follow, one at a time."

The members of the posse glanced at one another. All of them but one were western men, and they understood how Considine was thinking. Sure, he had made a big strike. He had sixty thousand in gold and a clear run to the border—but here was a man and a girl on one horse, with Indians on their trail...and they might not even know it.

The picture was plain: Considine had gone to help, and the others had followed him.

"That Dutch," Weedin said, "he's a good man, too."

"Well," Runyon said, and he turned his horse, "the men we want and the loot they took have gone up High Lonesome, so let's ride."

But Runyon contemplated the situation uneasily. He had that strong sense of justice and fairness that was so much a part of the western man, for it was the way of the time and the country to judge a man by his motives as well as by the results, and it was obvious that Considine and his outlaws had thrown over a chance for escape to help some people they could only have known casually, at best.

It would not be pleasant to arrest Considine after this, but they would have no choice. Arrest him, or shoot him.

Runyon swore quietly, and Weedin turned to look at

120

him. "Ollie, that damned fool could have whipped me. He let up on me—twice."

"Maybe."

"That's what makes me so mad. He was playing with me!"

"Wouldn't say that," Weedin commented dryly. "I seen that fight. There wasn't much layin' back, no matter what you may think. Considine just needed time. He wasn't thinkin' of you. He was thinkin' of those boys at the bank."

Runyon merely growled. He was angry with himself. All through the fight he had known something was wrong, because Considine was not acting like himself. He was never one to taunt a man—whip him, yes, but not taunt him. Considine had been doing his best to get Runyon so mad he could not think clearly.

"Well," Weedin said mildly, "he's one of our own. It wasn't any damned outsider who done it."

Knowing the humor of the men who followed him, Runyon was aware that, angry as they were at being tricked, they were somewhat mollified by that fact: Considine was one of their own boys. There were men here, men like Weedin, who had fought Indians and punched cows beside Considine.

Epperson, who never missed a posse any more than he did a fight, pulled alongside of Runyon. "Pete, those Indians may beat us to it."

"Save us trouble," Eckles spoke up.

Epperson exchanged an irritated glance with Weedin. "I wouldn't wish that on any man," he said brusquely.

"Outlaws," Eckles responded. "What's the difference?"

Runyon touched a spur to his horse to step up the gait. Eckles was new out here. He didn't know what Apaches could do to a man. Eckles was all right, but he needed education.

121

The clouds were breaking up now, and the sun was coming through. It was going to be another hot day, hot and muggy after the rain. Runyon could smell the damp earth, the way it smelled when the rain came after a long dry spell.

These men were family men, most of them. They should be at home, he was thinking, not out here in Indian country chasing outlaws. How much was sixty thousand dollars, anyway? How many lives would it buy? How much sadness would it pay for if one of these men was killed?

Just then, somewhere in the distance, far up around High Lonesome, they heard a shot.

The sound hung in the still air, and each man sat his saddle a little straighter, but they did not look at each other. The shot was followed by the drum of rifle fire.

The thunder of far-off battle rolled down the canyon.

"What d'you think, Pete?"

"High Lonesome...they're making a stand on High Lonesome."

Suddenly silent, rifles ready, ears alert for the slightest sound, twenty-five belted men rode into the hard bright sunlight.

Hardy and Dutch...good men gone.

Considine walked around the small circle and gathered their weapons, stripping each body of its cartridge belt and pistol.

The Kiowa was rolling a smoke. There was blood on his face from a scalp wound that Lennie had tried to stop from bleeding. "I think we don't make it, hey?" the Kiowa said.

"Maybe."

Considine levered a shell into the chamber of Dutch's rifle and stood it against a boulder. A loaded rifle ready at hand could be almost as good as an extra man—but not quite.

122

"Kiowa...if they get me, kill Lennie."

"All right."

The Kiowa drew on his cigarette. There was a swelling over one eye, and Considine wondered what had happened out there during the night. "We make a good fight, hey? Many are kill," the Indian said.

They *were* making a good fight. These men around him, both the living and the dead, had used their guns many times before. They had fought Indians and killed buffalo. They had killed deer and mountain sheep and bear. They knew how to shoot, and when.

Considine looked down at the canyon. Where the hell was that posse? He wanted them desperately now, no matter what happened to him. He wanted Lennie to live. He wanted Spanyer and the Kiowa to live.

The trouble was you never could see an Indian until he came at you...at least not often. And the Indians would know what they had done. Trust them to know that two men were out of action, and that there was a girl in the circle. She was one reason for their persistence—the girl, and the weapons. For the Indians were always short of rifles and ammunition.

His eyes searched the grass, the brush, the trees. Two men were dead, and neither of them had needed to be here. They had come partly from loyalty to him; partly because of a young girl with a bright, fresh face who had smiled at them in her frank and friendly fashion; and partly because each of them was, to some degree, living the life of chivalry each admired in his secret heart.

No sound, no movement. The waiting was hell, almost worse than the end of waiting. An occasional touch of wind rustled the grass and the leaves. The clouds were broken, the sun was bright on the mountains. High Lonesome lay still under the morning sun.

Spanyer stepped up beside Considine. "You ain't just the man I might have picked—sort of wanted her married to some steady man who'd give her what she deserves, but if you get out of this, Considine, you have my blessing, for what it's worth."

"I'd like nothing better, Dave."

Get out? Who was going to get out?

Suddenly an Indian showed, climbing to the high rocks that overlooked their position. If an Indian got up there they would have no chance, none at all. The only reason the attackers had held off was that it was a dangerous climb.

Considine lifted his rifle. The Indian appeared out of the shelter of the treetops, climbing by hands and feet up the almost sheer face. Considine fired, and they saw his outstretched hand turn to a burst of crimson. The Indian started to slide back and Spanyer fired. The Indian humped his back strangely, then fell clear.

And then they came with a rush.

Considine dropped his rifle and opened up with his six-gun. He felt rather than heard the roaring of his gun, then flipped the gun to his left hand and caught his left-hand gun with the right in the border shift, continuing his firing.

Something hit him low and very hard, and he half turned. There was gun smoke before him and a savage face looming through it. He fired from where the gun was and saw the face wiped away as if by a mighty fist. The Indian fell back, pawing at the raw furrow where his eyes had been.

Considine wheeled to look at Lennie, and saw Spanyer fighting with a huge warrior, struggling for a knife. Considine turned swiftly and brought his gun down as though on a target and shot the Indian through the temple. He saw Spanyer's eyes turn toward him and then Considine himself was down, fighting in mortal combat with a stocky Indian—who smelled, of all things, of cheap perfume, probably captured in some raid.

Considine struggled up, and felt angry teeth tear at his side. He shot an Indian who was coming over the barrier, and saw the Kiowa fall to his knees, laying about him with a Bowie knife.

Then he saw the Kiowa start to come up, and three bullets seemed to strike him at once. He was knocked clear around and fell back against the rocks, and as he caught Considine's eyes on him, he seemed about to smile.

Just then Considine saw an Indian grasp Lennie, and he lunged up and stepped in swiftly, laying the long barrel of his six-shooter along the man's head. As the Indian fell, Considine shot into him.

His pistol knocked from his fist, Considine grasped the Bowie knife the Kiowa had dropped, and threw himself at the other Indians who were fighting around Lennie.

Right and left he slashed, his blade red. His shirt was torn from his body, but he fought like a man gone berserk, until the Indians fell away from him...and they fell back...and back....

He rushed out of the circle of rocks. He ran a few feet, searching right and left for an enemy to strike at. Something was wrong—he saw no Indians. He turned halfway around and heard Lennie call something to him, and she threw him a Winchester.

He caught it in midair, and then he was running—why or where he had no idea. He ran, and then he stumbled and fell with his face in the wet grass. He tried to get up, but could only crawl forward. He felt the shadow of brush around him, and crawled like an animal, deeper into the darkness. The last thing he could remember was Lennie screaming something at him.

What was she trying to say to him? Had it been a warning? And where were the Indians?

From somewhere he heard a vast thunder that seemed to come from the earth beneath him, a thunder that grew louder and then suddenly faded out, and he was alone. It was dark, and his memory was gone...Was this what it felt like to die?

The Obaro posse, led by Pete Runyon, came with a rush. They came spread out in a scattered line, and they came with a thunder of hoofs.

Racing up, guns ready, they rode into High Lonesome, but it was into a dead silence. The basin was empty. Hot stillness held itself in this hollow hand of hills.

Where there had been the beat of rifle fire, there was now no sound but that of the soft wind. High overhead a buzzard circled, soon to be joined by another.

They slowed to a funeral pace, for, wise in such things, they knew they rode into a place of death.

A lone gray gelding stood by a clump of mesquite. On the ground, abandoned by the fleeing Indians, were the dark, still forms of the Apache and Yuma dead.

The circle of rocks was before them...and within it...?

An old man appeared suddenly in an opening of the rocks, a bloody old man, and beside him a girl in a torn dress. A wide-eyed and frightened girl, but a pretty one, despite that.

"They had no sense, Pete," Weedin said. "They rode right into a fight they couldn't win."

Dave Spanyer and Lennie stood waiting. "Howdy," Spanyer said. "Ain't much to say except that you didn't come any too soon."

Pete Runyon looked past him into the ring of rocks, then walked his horse still closer. From the saddle he could see into the rough circle that had been their defensive position.

He saw a dead Apache, then Dutch, lying half under the rocks, a cartridge spilled on the ground near him. The Indian he had throttled lay beside him in death.

Dutch...the big man was wanted in seven states.

126

And Hardy…all whang leather and steel wire, tough, dangerous, quick to shoot. He lay where he had taken his last bullet. The gravel near his mouth was dark with blood.

"There's the money," Epperson said. He made no move to pick it up—just looked at it.

Eckles glanced around, saw the Kiowa sprawled and dead, and looked further. He started to speak, but Weedin interrupted.

"It must have been a buster of a fight. There's seventeen or eighteen dead Indians out there."

Weedin took a cautious look around. The other men looked away uneasily—at the sky, at the mountains. One man kicked his toe into the gravel, another cleared his throat.

"We'd better get out of here, Pete." Weedin's voice was casual. "They'll be coming back for their dead—with more Injuns."

Two of the men moved abruptly toward their horses, eager to be away. A third and a fourth followed. Most of the men had not dismounted.

Nobody looked toward the steeldust gelding.

"We might catch us a couple of those Apache horses," Spanyer commented. "We're goin' on to Californy."

"After *this?*"

"Where we was headed. Where we aim to go."

Eckles lifted a hand to point toward the gelding, but his eyes met Weedin's and his hand stopped in midair and he walked hastily away.

Pete Runyon picked up a sack of the gold and handed it to Weedin, then took the other himself. He stood looking around him, trying not to seem curious, but struggling to read the story in the earth, scarred with footprints and evidence of the struggle. Once, lifting his eyes, he glanced toward the brush against the wall of rock, some distance off.

127

"Nothin' over there," Dave Spanyer said quietly. "They came from the other way."

"These were outlaws," Runyon said. "They robbed the Obaro bank."

Dave Spanyer looked straight into his eyes. "Three of 'em, was there?"

"Why, yes." Pete Runyon spoke slowly. He had not considered that aspect. "There were just three."

At his horse, Runyon worked with the saddle. His canteen slipped and fell to the earth, but he ignored it. He stepped into the saddle. "You and your daughter," he said, "you come with us. We'll see you started on your way."

Dave Spanyer mounted the horse they brought for him. Lennie, her face very pale, was already in the saddle. She kept her eyes on the horizon, as if there was something out there that gripped her attention...or as if she dared not trust herself to look anywhere else.

Spanyer glanced at Weedin and Murphy, both of them seasoned with dust and fighting and the ways of men and cattle. "They come just in time, those outlaws. Only just in time," he said.

"They done some shootin'," Weedin said.

The posse turned their horses and started down from High Lonesome. Runyon looked over at Weedin. "You got some tobacco, Ollie?"

"Sure haven't, Pete. Must've lost mine...back there."

They rode away down the canyon and nobody wanted to look back. After a few minutes Lennie and Dave Spanyer caught up with them.

"Our bank was robbed," Murphy commented, to no one in particular, "but we've got nothing to be ashamed of."

No sound disturbed the clear air of afternoon. Wind stirred in the grass, ruffling the hair of a dead Apache.

Out from the brush against the rock wall crawled a

tall, lean-waisted young man and he limped toward the steeldust, that somehow had his bridle caught in the brush. There was blood on Considine's leg, and there was blood on his side, but he could walk, and he carried his rifle.

A gun belt with his six-shooters hung over the pommel of the steeldust's saddle. Considine found the canteen where it had been dropped, with the name on the side in black paint...*Pete.* He saw the sack of tobacco, and retrieved it.

Once more in the saddle, he took the trail the Kiowa had used and rode up into the hills above High Lonesome.

Far off to the east, on the main trail, he saw a small dark spot, and a trailing dust cloud—the posse, returning home with the bodies of three dead outlaws.

On the hill's long crest he sat his horse, the sun in his eyes. There was a stubble of beard on his jaws. He was weak from loss of blood and very tired, but he scarcely glanced toward the south and the border. Castle Dome lifted its massive shoulders above the desert mountains.

Shadows, faintly purple, were gathering along the mountains. Far off, the Sand Tanks were already growing darker. He started the steeldust down the hill toward the west, toward California.

There would be no riding with the wind out there, no wild dashes for safety and freedom. There would be hard, driving work, with something building and growing around him, and there would be a girl who had held herself still in his arms, looking up at him, waiting for something within him to respond, something he had forgotten was there.

He moved his wounded leg, easing the pad he had made over the wound, and walked his horse away.

Behind him the wind stirred the grass, and the hills that had waited so long in silence had already forgotten their brief moments of blood and battle. The echoes had disappeared into the canyons and lost themselves there, the smell of gunpowder was gone...the grass remained.

The gray horse walked steadily, and the face of the man called Considine lost its strain. Down there on the flat, only a few miles west, an old man and a girl were waiting, as they had said they would wait.

Behind him the wind moved down from High Lonesome, but only the wind blew along the trails, south to the border, south to Mexico.